The Too-Brief Chronicle of Judah Lowe

Christopher Carter Sanderson

Cover design by Royce M. Becker.
Set in Adobe Garamond with LaTeX.

ISBN: 978-0-9861445-4-7 (paperback)
ISBN: 978-0-9861445-6-1 (ebook)

Sagging Meniscus Press
web: http://www.saggingmeniscus.com/
email: info@saggingmeniscus.com

For Andre

Foreword

The unusual form of this novel calls for some explanation. In 2012, Esquire Magazine ran a writing contest in honor of its 79th anniversary with the rule that each story submitted be exactly 79 words long. With a characteristic mixture of whimsy and audacity, Christopher Carter Sanderson was inspired by this challenge to write *79/79/'79*, a novella set in the year 1979, with 79 titled chapters, each 79 words in length. If the editors at Esquire were nonplussed when this little epic was fired across their masthead, it did not matter; Sanderson serialized the work on Facebook.

At just this time, several writers of note happened to issue, on social media, dire-sounding pronouncements about the pernicious impact of social media on literature. Sanderson's response was to demonstrate his faith in their creative possibilities by continuing the story he had begun in *79/79/'79* with *@1000thenovel*, a novel in 1000 tweets, broadcast on the Twitter account of the same name. The numerological play continued: not only is each of those tweets 140 characters long, but the novel itself has a cast of 140 characters.

The serialization of the story caught on, and the author carefully planned out the schedule of his forthcoming tweets, staging them in groups, considering how they would appear in the midst of his subscribers' Twitter feeds. As *@1000thenovel*'s following grew, however, it became apparent that it was awkward for new readers, coming in in the middle, to go back and read from the beginning, as Twitter showed tweets only in reverse chronological order. The work cried out for being presented in a more readable form, joined with its prequel. That is the origin of the book you hold in your hands.

But while that origin story explains the circumstances that led to the author's choice of these forms, it does not explain what potential he saw in them and what special use he made of them. For there is nothing arbitrary about the wedding here of formal constraint with subject matter; the spine-like construction of the book from self-contained fragments caught in a long arc is just what the story, and the adolescent experience of its protagonist, demands. There is something about even its visual structure, by virtue of it being made of so many small sections, that evokes a kind of childlike fantasy, greatly appealing to a reader who loves the sense of exploration and repletion that comes with lists and catalogues; such a book is like a playhouse with a thousand rooms, in each, a different life to be lived. And in this sense of a myriad possibilities and alternate futures, and of paths between them, we encounter the unity of the book's form and its subject. For in this *Bildungsroman*, a boy in high school discovers the world, the soul of the Other, and himself, crystallized again and again in one manifestation after another. Each little story or tweet is a more or less separate universe with its own perfect balance and completeness; each experience is a more or less separate thing that includes its own, more or less necessary or automatic, response. Each window lets out onto a different chamber of the world, with infinite possibilities in every direction. And gradually, the protagonist gets the hang of something crucial – that creative choice exists not only within these tiny spheres of intense action and reaction, but in moving between them, in creating a life. From the multifariousness of experience, he discovers the singularity of human freedom, and launches forth into the unknown.

The protagonist, you will find, is not the Judah Lowe named in the title (which is also the title of a book written within the book, for the voice of the Twitter author *@1000thenovel* is a character too), but is one Moe (short, I like to fancy, for *Monad*). Judah is an overwhelming personal influence, a companion, inspiration, and leader, whose intense friendship, and subsequent withdrawal of it, act on Moe like the gravitational attraction of a sun on a rocket, that almost pulls it into its orbit and then flings it on a long mission. It is not for nothing that this secondary figure is named after the Rabbi who, it is said, created the Golem of Prague, and at a certain point ceased to be able to control him. Judah's influence was decisive, but Moe invites many influences into his life and sensibility, and absorbs something from each of them. The refreshing plurality of his world is full of the love for all the intense, idiosyncratic manifestations of human life.

There are two other omnipresent but unnamed characters in this chronicle, hinted in all the titles and numerology: Time itself, its installments numbered, always too brief; and a time, 1979, 1980, or thereabouts, whose flesh and spirit are captured in concrete detail, with no false patina of nostalgia, but with the deep reverence of observant memory. Conceived together, as in this remarkable novel, the eternal and the transient may make us feel that as the past is radically specific, mortal, and lovable, so is the present and the future.

—Jacob Smullyan

Contents

79/79/'79

1. The Brothers Tazwell

Young Tazwell tossed the anchor from their family's small boat up over the fake-gothic crenellations of the High School theatre building, its nylon line un-spooling at his feet. Moe frowned as he grabbed a hearty twist of the line and smiled. Hand over hand, he ascended. Taz imitated his brother's walk up the wall. Next morning, Principal Jameson opened his office door and hundreds of white mice scampered out beneath his coffee cup and into the brightening hallways.

2. The Anatomy of Courage

He walked to the center of the lawn, having marched right out of the tenth-grade History class he was teaching. Mr. Locker was thinking of his bowels, his ass from the inside, and all of the fluids in his body in a way that would have been embarrassing if he wasn't so terrified. And the box would be found by the State Bomb Squad to have contained: a bundle of road flares, some old phone wires and a clock.

3. Alice, Exposed

Alice was talking, there on the only benches in that vast yard in front of school. A field-hockey player, all strong thighs and skirt. You'd think she was talking to herself. Moe lay, hidden by the bulk of his bench, the folds of his oversize black coat, and his round, blue sunglasses, listening to his hangover, only vaguely registering her plaintive, round face. It was talked about with giggles for days; she remembered it with anger for years.

4. Dodecahedron

I would decide you had gotten under the suspended sculpture that Jason left in his garage to see it centered on its face instead of the vortex. I'd ask you on Facebook. You'd never get back to me. You were probably building robots again. That day, in that garage, it was we who felt controlled from the inexorable outside. The wreck that was left of Jason and his car had no such symmetry. Then, we went to the movies.

5. Cri de Coeur

Reuben, rail thin 6'5" in a deerstalker hat, wandered into the meeting of the Alternative Literary Magazine, scrawled on the blackboard in Ancient Greek, next discussing writers we'd never heard of. In orchestra class he flawlessly executed a piano sonata. The night of the State Orchestra Final, we pulled him away from feverishly practicing on the edge of his hotel bed, reeking of vodka. We thought he was asleep in his underwear, when he cried out, "Liszt! Liszt! REALITY!"

6. Chess

Oh, a poem and a drawing of chessmen tumbling from the page, changing shape, flying away. Her bright eyes, smile, childish voice, all on the cusp. Her black hair and pale skin. As if summoned by his hopes, she walked up. The Rapidograph pen was so perfect, the lines so fine, a professional magic wand from the temple in New York City ... Pearl Paint. "I always say, those Tazwell brothers sure can draw." And then ... she just ... walked away.

7. The Socratic Method

It left the indelible image of Socrates as an aging, German-looking High School teacher in an improbable black toupée. The rules were: you read the one-page purple mimeograph, and then spent the rest of the class questioning Mr. Davits as if he were Socrates. The questions got unexpectedly racy right through wine, sex and the *Symposium*. And then, Socrates' question for us: if we were drinking Christ's blood and eating his body every Sunday, didn't that make us cannibals?

8. Rather the Bass in Hell…

His mother played the record of each instrument, solo, over and over. Moe said, "I'd like to play the bass." She took up the needle and said, "you're seven, too short for the bass. How about the cello? My favorite!" Junior year, the competition landed him at second deck in the cello section of the orchestra. Looking down at the end-pin he'd had lengthened twice now, he walked out during the Telemann. His first bass lesson was that afternoon.

9. Suicide

No, it was not a good idea. They kissed, seriously. No, it was not a good idea. They were sitting in the window alcove known as "Moe's office" at school in broad daylight. No, it was not a good idea. His girlfriend would not understand. No, it was not a good idea. She had decided to commit suicide. Yes, it was a great idea. He said, "I just think you should use a slower method, like champagne. Or cigarettes."

10. Away

No way. The Keither was not going to steal the school flag. Not going to happen. That was OK. The Keither could still hang around. No big deal. McTierney High School awaited the next plot. For one thing, nobody had packed a car full and run in to Greenwich Village in way too long. Just as they pulled out, The Keither dove in across the back-seat laps. And all the way there, the school flag streamed out the window.

11. That Day

They moved into their new house, in this new town. It wouldn't last; they'd be in a cheaper one by the time school was out. The movers rushed. They gave her five bucks to help with small things and direct traffic. Voyager 11 sent pictures of Jupiter's rings. She assembled her new chair. Spacelab began to fall to earth. She had a fever of 103 when they lifted her into bed. That day, Jen turned 13: March 4, 1979.

12. A Melancholy Age

The loved youngest boy of a family of boys, it was Junior Year and he had everything: that bright red chariot of his childhood desires – his eldest brother's car – and the beta tapes of Hornblower, favorite of all the boys, lawn darts and a huge lawn, a pool, the aging, happy family dog: everything. There was everything five boys could want, except four of the boys. The youngest of his older brothers would graduate college this year.

13. Chick 'n Bones

Jess could make surplus Army pants look really, really … that. Joyous, free, essential on the field hockey team, dancing in the middle of every party like the nymph spirit of cool. She was staring dreamily into space. Turning the corner, Moe saw the large pile of bones on the curb. His eyebrows made a question mark and Jess just sighed, smiled and said, "he's such an animal." Years later, he'd find out Jess had become a US Forest Ranger.

14. An Angel Popped Up

After guns, the pale kid would talk about playing the harmonica. Rumors went around. He was abused; the empty Jack Daniels bottles stacked in the drainage grate were his, and so on. Sad, so full with something he wasn't telling. Moe brought out a tall bass from the orchestra room to the smoking wall. Once through a 12-bar, twice. Then, the kid looked distant, pulled out that harmonica and played. Better than the radio, better than anything mortal.

15. Decontextual Fries

Like a nightmare sloppy zombie Big Mac imitation, nobody ever finished a Big Duke. They filled the cafeteria garbage cans with oozing sludge. On a bad day the french-fries were all that was edible. Even so, your fingers would stink of cooking oil, no matter how you scrubbed them in the Boy's Room. A murmur started up, then laughter. Taz had a pair of chopsticks from the local takeout and was calmly eating fries. They never touched his fingers.

16. The New World

One day, she woke up and walked into town. Light streamed up from the fresh snow on the ground. She had never worn this coat in Atlanta. She walked onto the college campus, a phony Disney version of Oxford or Cambridge built in the '30's, and it captivated her. She wandered inside and moved down the hall. Nobody stopped her. Some of them looked younger than she. Jen sat through a whole lecture: The Discovery of the New World.

17. A Liszt of Friends

Hung over and mortified behind the grim peak of his nose, Reuben strode onstage to polite applause from the judges. The deep breath he took seemed to focus his intensity on the piano. In fact, he couldn't remember even the first note. He looked up, and saw that the bass players had put their hats on top of their basses. Among them, Reuben's deerstalker flew like a tweed flag. Reuben exhaled, and his long hands went to their place.

18. Protest Poems

Animal Farm, then on to *1984*, *Brave New World*, *Fahrenheit 451*, *A Clockwork Orange*, and *Lord of the Flies*. A mirthless march lead by teachers unaware of the parallels to what was between their classroom walls. Words, words, words. And then they were weapons. Anonymous poems appeared, Xeroxed from handwritten originals and taped to the walls. What was incredible was that they were talked about by the busy hordes rushing by to class; and that they weren't taken down.

19. Flight

Jon-O and Mike were going to be fighter pilots, I tell you. They read about flying, talked about flying, and they calculated and performed precision maneuvers with their ten-speeds. The front wheel of Tim's bike would glide by the rear wheel of Jon-O's with millimeters to spare. Then they would wheel around for the opposite. They conducted pre- and post-flight briefings. I think Jon-O's garage really looked like an aircraft carrier briefing room. Tim's mom could never, ever know.

20. Moe's Message

Never, ever forget that this was hard. Never look back on this with nostalgia; this is not sweet nonsense. This is a message to my future self. Remember: I'm wearing a yellow button-down shirt, sitting in the empty theater. Like performing dogs acting out their master's delusions, the Drama Club has performed a High School musical. Evil. Wrong. Future self, I put this message in your memory from who you were now: Never, ever forget this was hard.

21. King Tut

Alex got into the city every weekend that April. His sense of expectation was always as starched as his chinos. The weekend train, so empty. The tomb's contents, he listed them quietly to himself. The names of the goddesses in their skin-tight dresses, still so chic after 3,000 years. Look, he thought, maybe it was OK to have big lips, narrow eyes and skin that was, if you looked at it just right reflected in that train window, gold.

22. Tazwell Bros., Inc.

McCoy loves you long enough to find out what's hip, then he buys it and drops you. Sometimes, he lucks into it. The Village is cool? His mom writes for the Voice. Driving in? His BMW is already there. Clothes? You shop cheap in the East Village, he snaps it up next day. Score a sack of hemp from your hillbilly uncle? McCoy steals it from the party. His BMW never recovered from that potato up its tailpipe, though.

23. Division

Four of them came to school ready to head out on Friday: black suits, white shirts, thin ties, and sharp shoes. Nobody razzed McCoy for dressing up too. They were just looking forward to a party. They weren't late for math class, they were early. They chatted up friends, and had forgotten the fun of all the mod gear. The math teacher handed out the mimeographed test, and instead of explaining, blurted out, "so, what are you guys? Undertakers?"

24. What's On Display

At this point, the Museum of Natural History on the college campus is a display of outdated ideas, not scientific facts. An ugly mural is valued because of its age and not because of any fidelity to the Age of the Dinosaurs. It shows big Godzillas running around instead of Tyrannosaurus Rexes. Nobody cares. The Polar Bear unmarked is therefore not a victim of error. Crummy stuffed Eskimos peer at Moe and smirk at the inappropriateness of their display.

25. March 28, 1979

Peach Bottom, Browns Ferry, Millstone, Crystal River, Vermont Yankee… summer camps, places your kindly great aunt might live, or friendly train lines? "Vermont Yankee now boarding for fly-fishing spots," perhaps. You might like a few days at "Millstone" B&B or a dip in "Crystal River." Sounding more like a preppy vacation enclave, Three Mile Island was a nuclear reactor, the first on this list to break. Jen felt guilty – glad of the cover – slipping into her new school.

26. Alien Logic

Aliens from outer space would think that nuclear reactors this crude should be kept three miles underground. Nobody should have to die to get inside them if they break. Two-lane roads were insane to the aliens, with inches between cars speeding at each other. Jason would have found the essay funny; as it was Moe didn't get into Honors English with it and was often asked why. He told the curious to ask Mrs. Keny about her alien logic.

27. The Pangloss Papers

The beef between the school's literary magazine and its "alternative literary magazine" was not so much a true rivalry as a sequestration. It kept the quiet, approved, achieving kids – the kids who wanted to please – away from the outright intellectual and creative brawl that was considered "alternative." There had been ACLU lawsuits. Each year brought Principal Jameson's personal attention to issues of its content. Thirty years later, every kid in it was a published, employed writer or artist.

28. The Optimist

Charlie, a gangly, straw-haired freshman who sang the blues with a big heart, could play his own cool songs too. Starting with the cafe under the college's religion building, everyone asked him back once they'd heard him. Moe called Charlie "my once-a-month friend" because every month, they'd pick him up and he'd sing sweet, play the guitar and be free for one night. Then they'd drop Charlie off and he'd be screamed at and grounded again for another month.

29. And where there is despair, may we bring hope...

Later, the election-winning idea of replacing the school cafeteria with a MacDonald's would happen, if not at McTierney. A last-minute notion, as indeed Moe's nomination to the ballot for Student Representative to the School Board had been, it was just sheer luck to be the last thing said by the last person to speak. Other candidates had better notes, better ideas, better speeches. But, the bored, annoyed students erupted at the idea that lunch could actually be worth eating.

30. In Mind of Etan Patz

That little boy was still missing in the city. Tim hoped he'd be OK as he walked through the rain to the bus stop. Two towns over, a walk across the parking lot – empty now, it would be packed with Cameros. The boss insisted he be early. Would the cool kids at the roller-disco ever suspect that it was him, a skinny 14-year-old, behind the smoked glass of that DJ booth? Lucky his voice had changed last year.

31. Burning Basses

Like a patrol of young WW1 soldiers somehow, with tweed caps instead of *Pickelhauben*, in long black coats and formal shoes, the entire bass section of the school orchestra marched across the virgin snow – or like a strange murder of crows or the large black tone-clusters on a white page of modern music. The rest of the instruments had fit into cars for the ride across the field to the Middle School. But passion was a warm fuel.

32. "I did not bow down to you, I bowed down to all the suffering of humanity"

"The cat's out of the bag" means you've already been found guilty and the cat-o-nine-tails is out of its leather bag to give you your lashes. The author of the Protest Poems had so far remained anonymous. Their latest hit was a flight of metaphor only clear in that it was about the Vice Principal. So it wasn't to the principal's office that Moe was sent after sitting down in gym class to pen a poem against compulsory fun.

33. The Scarlet Letters

The answer was "no" and should have stayed that way. In a moment of weakness, assailed on two sides by attractive, earnest representatives of the literary magazine and yearbook for quotes, Moe broke down. It was the last possible moment. If you read the capitalized first letters of the hasty poem for the magazine, they spelled EAT SHIT. The yearbook's … even worse. He circled them in red ink at the end of year for anyone who wanted a signature.

34. In Medias Res

The kid flew around the track, pacing the blond twins in their matching track uniforms. They were here from Germany, the stars of every meet. Gym class was a mere rehearsal of their glory. This kid, in faded jeans with a peacock feather flying behind his ear was not slowing down. He was barefoot. In the last twenty yards, he sprinted away, yards ahead of them and kept going, toward the open road. Why wasn't he on the team?

35. "We cannot...substitute myths for common sense"

I Ran From Iran When The Shooting Began and *Bomb Iran*. Jon-O had them both on cassette. He'd saved up for a Walkman. All of the pro-wrestling heroes had turned from Sputnik Monroe to Arab-looking caricatures. In the background, droning news footage of serious-looking men talking soberly about destroying America. They really seemed to mean what they were saying. Moe couldn't find a response to their ideas. Hell, Moe couldn't find one single person who was taking them seriously.

36. The Temple

Their patron saint, Mrs. Cecily, helped them dare to have a Student Composers Club at McTierney High. Milton Babbitt's new atonalism, graduate student computerized electronic music, and the Medieval Music Society on the college campus, sometimes all in one night. They survived brutal humiliation to get to the meetings. Oh, sonorous joy, Mrs. Cecily would have the school orchestra play what they wrote. She delighted in surprising audiences by saving the composer's name until after the successful performance.

37. The Story of Drake and the Motorcycle

The red lights of the motorcycle faded into the night. Moe couldn't find Drake after the performance. He hadn't even taken a bow. This was just supposed to be a High School performance of *The Zoo Story*. But, it was superlative, amazing. Held the whole school, electrified. Word had gotten out, somehow. Some thought to see the fat loser kid fall apart. He hadn't. It changed people. Kids that night decided on the spot that incredible things were possible.

38. Both

Taz was changing. Angry outbursts that he didn't remember. He would get strident about things. It wasn't like him. It got worse. Tim recommended a counselor to Moe and he went. He couldn't drag his parents along. Taz wasn't going. Untangling this from the giant knot called "teen" seemed impossible. McTierney High School didn't help; the peer counselors were supposed to be perfect. They got to be superior by pretending they had no problems. Moe was one of them.

39. Brooklyn Brobdingnagian

Giant, and his vitriol huge, a vocabulary of onomatopoetic bleats made you laugh even before you knew what they meant in Yiddish. Outsized opinions on everything, including the deification of The Mets and the special place in Hell for Jews of Judah's stripe (what that was, we were not sure). Noah towered, glowered, and glared down the school bullies. If trusted, you'd see the perfect, tiny soldiers he made. They looked on Noah's giant fingers with expressions completely individual.

40. Quite Early One Morning

Never was there such a lame school as ours, so weak and mean and smelling of industrial cleaners, with the foul and mumbled music of the Latin lessons echoing down from the second floor to the wall where the cigarettes were smoked, where only the wicked stood over undone lives, or to hide from punishment — better here than beaten in the geography class, or the damage done before investigation in English. Here, you could read Dylan Thomas in peace.

41. Now and Then

Moe knew the world's name: it was "New York." Otherwise known as "Oz," Manhattan was the Emerald City since his dad had brought back improbable toys from where the Wizard lived: FAO Schwartz. He got there when he could. Not old enough to drive, but the train left from the middle of town. There was no "junior" and "senior" there. Kitchen workers at Sweet Basil left the back door open. You could hear the jazz from a milk crate.

42. Turnabout is Airplay

Jen had seen *The Warriors* and hated New York. She would rather hear organ concerts at the Choir College and rebuff Moe's advances after teasing him long enough to make it hurt. Moe and Judah wrote a rock song for the radio contest. Her vanity got the better of her. After recording his mandolin track Moe left to see *All That Jazz* and wasn't there to hear her vocal track. She was too hurt to guard against showing it.

43. A Taste of Heaven

There were no teachers out looking. Taz walked toward Gyro Heaven and kept walking, expecting every second to get stopped. He had spent a half-hour deciding between a souvlaki and a cheese-steak when he'd first discovered the place. Not now: instant souvlaki, and forever souvlaki. He'd be in and out of institutions, but still find ways to visit this place again. One time, decades later, Moe would separate the parts of a souvlaki and FedEx them to Taz.

44. Nothing Down

The threadbare parts of the collar could not be denied. Carefully, he razored apart the yolk, lifted out the frayed part and stitched it back together. With two buttons still for the missing collar, he put it on. In Latin class, he forgot to cover it with his scarf. The red-haired trumpet player asked, "how did you get that collar?" Tim told him, ready to be humiliated. But next day, the entire brass section had sliced off their collars.

45. Touch Sensitive

Rainy and cold, it was a good night for coffee and conversation under the religion building on campus. Expecting the usual mix of majors ready to argue about God into the night and oddballs up for spontaneous art, they were all taken aback by the new knot of students, music stand, and better speakers than they'd ever seen. The young man set a guitar on that music stand to play with both hands on the fingerboard. It was uncanny.

46. Meliores te sumus

Unusual for a public High School for have a rugby team, even a club team. A crew team was unheard of. Some of the rugby players put together a boat with the help of the amateur club on the lake, though. They couldn't compete in any ranked race, but every private school in the area wanted to put them down. So they wore their t-shirts proudly emblazoned with a fake crest and Latin motto, often beaten but never shamed.

47. Cadenza

In a fit, Moe took the strings off of a short-necked electric bass, doctored the spacing and put on steel cello strings in cello tuning. He played Baroque music through a distortion box with the classical guitar-players who borrowed electrics for the occasion, or who secretly had them and brought them out of hiding. Even Marcus, musical polymath and Interlochen veteran, approved and nobly took it up to toss off a few Bach riffs with a rakish air.

48. Francis of Assisi

Everything in that clean, wood-paneled recording studio was in perfect condition, ready to work, and completely outdated. Judah and Moe were not Brian Eno. Still, they were High School students who thought $50 was a lot of money. So the old Catholic man who made nature films for schools showed them footage of animals fighting each other and then all afternoon they improvised – Judah on fretless bass and Moe on the electric cello now amazingly paying for itself.

49. Skin

Tom Wolfe on the cover of Esquire Magazine in front of a jet fighter. If only Taz could be that cool. Fly this like a fighter. Stride through this in a white suit. Her skin was perfect, like some buttery tan liquid poured over her lithe frame. Not Taz's. He needed to be here in this office, and the prescription to tame the volcanoes of his acne. Why did her dad have to be the only dermatologist in town?

50. Stop and Start

Moe's ten-speed flew out ahead, and he thought he'd left the older kids he didn't know far behind. But, he hadn't. They were racing to catch up. He hesitated, and stopped to wait and see. The two older kids flew around the corner, and Judah's bike scraped Moe's, and scraped Moe, and scraped Judah. There was pain, there was blood, but for some reason Judah Lowe and Moe Tazwell were inseparable after that for just over one perfect year.

51. The Valkyrie

Let the world sing of Liz. Rapture in her room, something sweet to look forward to between the beatings and razzings at school. Tim would skip class to peek into the orchestra room and see her, so earnest in the flute section. She loved Classical Music. He mounted the roller-disco DJ booth that night and spun a set like no other, building to a crescendo topped off by *Ritt der Walküren*. And, he was fired on the spot.

52. Navil

His mother clutched the banister. Her wild eyes were bright with truth. She spent most of her time in her room. Revelation was nigh. They had been in the kitchen; she was waiting. They froze, caught. "Be careful!" she hissed, "that Jon-O is … I don't want anyone to hear … that Jon-O … don't let him in here …" Then, with a sudden fortissimo, "He's a Nazi spy!" With that, she retreated. The boys, stunned, considered Jon-O: blonde, blue-eyed … and Jewish.

53. Law French

McCoy couldn't purchase the admiration DiNozzo commanded. When DiNozzo and McCoy's sister broke up, you could tell McCoy wanted to declare war, but on what? People liked Antonio. His football skill, handsome face and gold Camero should have added up to one major asshole – but they didn't. He really cared about people. McCoy made snide remarks about the Camero in public. In private, his pillow talk with Mandy became a tiresome ad hominem monologue. McCoy became a lawyer.

54. The Scoop

But everyone went to The Fred, town and gown. The Fredericks Ice Cream Shop, called "The Fred," made its own flavors. This was the claim. Tubs of ice cream were brought in late at night. No matter. Lines went around the block on hot nights. A young couple could find a table to watch the snow fall outside. But the summer line was social, and a job scooping at The Fred was a McTierney High School badge of status.

55. Night Train

Over twenty years later, Moe would make this hike after 1 in the morning, but that was 9/11 and another story. Tonight, he'd stayed late in The Village chasing Petal around NYU. She'd laughed a lot, mostly at him. The three-mile campus train had stopped running for the night. He walked the dark tracks through the woods and over trellises to the station, hopping up on the platform. A phalanx of bikes, some years abandoned, stood guard. He sympathized.

56. The Heat

That 1969 Pontiac convertible sure looked more than ten years old. The Texas vanity plates were wired on. Drake had dinner over. Moe borrowed the atlas, Taz jumped up on the passenger seat with a pair of binoculars. They drove all night. Down at Drake's cousin's farm there was a swimmin' hole, gangs of unruly relatives, cookouts, and relief. Sunday back, this time in broad daylight. The following week Drake got pulled over: farewell to childhood and that Pontiac.

57. Blockheads

Petal was nervous or didn't want to talk about something. She sang the funky songs she liked. How many boys had been introduced to Ian Dury this way? He didn't wander off, and she didn't leave and maybe that was something. Or not. More lyrics. Back home, the lone Gingko tree had turned yellow and left a magic golden halo around itself. He stepped reverently, as if into a sepulcher, to slowly slam his brow against the unyielding trunk.

58. No Exit

Fortune may favor the bold, the drunk, and maybe the young. Drake's decision to make a last-minute entry in the school's one-act festival was all three, really. Emily was so refined, a young woman of substance and grace. As Inez, she was sophisticated. They soldiered on through the philosophy, the sex, the language. Drake couldn't find a way out of his ignorance of what "mulatto" meant, or even how to pronounce it. "Mulatto," the lovely Emily said, "like me."

59. Bellerophon

It was a huge surprise when Tim's dad came home in the family station wagon with "a surprise" in the back. His business associate had gotten rid of this Italian moped, cheap. Not French and not small like everyone else's; it wasn't even worth trying to catch Tim to hurl some nasty bon mot. Tim bought extra mirrors. On the long, cold drive down the hill from Liz's he gazed up at Orion and saluted the cold, lonely warrior.

60. Magister Musicae

Ode and sonnet to Mrs. Cecily,
Her majestic, radiant, foxy grin.
Productive rehearsal moved easily;
Youthful musicians yearning to begin.
Musical conversation resounding,
Kind patience with the problematical,
Her bright, lovely humor abounding,
Inspiring even the fanatical.
Rewarding our hard efforts with knowledge,
Egalitarian though commanding,
Treating us more like we were in college,
We hardly saw that she was demanding.
Our compliments would paint a blush on her.
Could you blame those who had a crush on her?

61. Far Away

This band was everything, criticized everything Moe had loved and been dropped by. The lead singer was a senior in college, but the drummer had just graduated from McTierney High School last year. It was tall, funky proof that you could be a professional artist. It was hope you could dance to. They played NYC. They put magic in McTierney's gym. That lead singer would go on to live an artist's life of music while managing Haiti's Hotel Trianon.

62. Change

Taz had a handful of Susan B. Anthony dollars. The manager's sister worked for the Post Office and he had seen them. Taz was early for the matinee of *Apocalypse Now.* He let the little clear tab of LSD melt on his tongue like the guy had said to. You could trade a lot of things for a bong made out of forgotten biology class equipment. His evolution wasn't scary. What terrified him was that no one noticed it.

63. Tragedy

This new girl would never go out with Drake. She was clear about that. Moe was to promise never to date her anyway. A cheerleader back home in the South, she was the instant star of the Drama Club. Drake had never asked Moe for a favor before. He was emphatic about that and about demanding this one now. He deserved some hope. True. Moe still never saw any of it coming, and it all turned out so badly.

64. The Lost Weekend

Moe would give up drugs. It was a big thing with Judah. Not before a weekend with McCoy. They made a great study of Casteneda's books, and fasted all day Friday. McCoy said it was tiresome to wait for his mushrooms to work. Jamie watched TV. McCoy and Moe played chess. Next morning, mist rose over the back yard forming jolly cherubim, while the abandoned chess table stood with its pieces pushed together, strewn with hot pink flower petals.

65. Echo and Narcissus

Mandy was distraught. It was the end of the day. The school's halls were full. One by one, McCoy stopped people and asked them about Mandy. Anything unusual? His tone grew more insistent. McCoy: "Anything about the way she's dressed?" Moe: "She looks nice. Mandy, you look nice today." Mandy: "Nice today?" No, that wasn't OK. Mandy had dressed preppy and it was supposed to be ironic. But nobody understood that. Mandy and McCoy were made for each other.

66. Eat Me

Drake was tired and it must have shown. Waiting for rehearsal to start, too broke to get a snack. Joyous Jess bounded in, "I made special brownies!" She had saved one for him. So sweet and slightly spicy. Halfway through rehearsal, the lights went bright. Then, darkness. Drake looked up from the basement where he had fallen, bloody, pulled himself out, and must have walked home. The next day, Jess said, "You ate the whole thing at once?"

67. American Revolution

Petal's father was English. Moe thought this boded well. Many nights, he and Taz had crept halfway down the stairs as soon as they heard *Sinfonies de Fanfares: Rondeau.* Their anglophile parents were absorbed in the BBC's Masterpiece Theatre. Forbidden pleasure had an English accent. Her father was distant, remarried now. Not too distant to call their dad at 4 in the morning to ask, "don't you think they are being rather too intimate?" Perhaps anger shouldn't fuel desire.

68. Pax Romana

A handsome actor named Patrick Stewart played Lucius Aelius Sejanus in the BBC's *I, Claudius.* Cultivating power then undone by his own hubris, his body tossed down the Gemonian stairs. Moe had summarily turned down the presidency of the High School orchestra, debate team, drama club, alternate literary magazine, a nomination to the presidency of the student council. Petal just said, "I'm just not interested any more." The steps of the New York Public Library were there for Moe.

69. Poem Number Sixty-Nine

The bus to Liz's mom's apartment was always sweet, but today turned serious. The future was in their hands, and Tim looked down at his a lot. He hadn't asked about sex in a while. It only hung in the air now because her twin sister had done it with that soccer player, a college guy. "I asked my counselor and he said he couldn't think of any difference between sex and what we already do, so why not?" Joy.

70. Wasting Lives

By Christmas, Jon-O could play Asteroids forever on a single quarter. He would line up extra lives across the screen. He even wasn't allowed in the dark Greek pizza places any more. We took the bus to the roller rink where he could play all night. He could roll to the bathroom and back while you wasted lives for him. Jon-O wanted to be a fighter pilot until he started smoking pot. Then, he wanted to be a carpenter.

71. Late Nights

At Judah's house, bagels were like chewing gum. Fretted, picked apart. His dad's small screen had bright green letters and brought furtive messages from the kids of other professors. The big suction cups would squeal, then Judah would bury the phone in them. His dad would talk about relativity, or about computers. He liked Judah's idea that, someday, a computer would be as small as a notebook. You'd be able to carry it around. They chewed it all over.

72. Geometry of Circles

Jess asked Drake because they were in fifth grade together. Drake asked Tim because he was good in science. Tim asked Noah because he knew everything. Noah asked Judah though they rarely spoke. Judah, embarrassed, asked Jon-O. Jon-O asked Mike easily. Mike asked Alex because he was Black, too, or at least half. Alex asked Taz, Taz asked his brother Moe, of course. The sexiest person he could think of must know all about sex, so Moe asked Jess.

73. Ellipsis

Like a Mad Lib in Spanish, her homework had carefully underlined blank spaces where a word was still missing, sometimes a phrase. Tim helped Liz look them up. Between kisses, he could make her laugh by filling in the remaining blanks with improbable words in funny voices. She read the finished passages out with a proud Castilian lisp. It seemed that they said so much in those blank spaces. But she would never, ever tell him what really happened.

74. Solo

Something incredible was coming, as the smokers at the wall knew. The end- of-year School Jazz Band recital, before they left for the contests, and the kid was getting up to do a solo. He did. He looked confused. You could read his lips: the harmonica was in the wrong key. The bandleader shrugged. The band played on. The kid looked distant. And then he bent it back into the right key with blazing thirty-second-note runs to a standing ovation.

75. Language and Responsibility

Drake had convinced the printer to charge it to the school's account, but that wasn't cash in hand. And there were buyers waiting. The battle-lines had been drawn for weeks. Mr. Jameson couldn't stop the printing, but he could ban the sale inside school buildings. So that bright afternoon saw Drake at a card table in the middle of the lawn, flanked by a white-haired ACLU lawyer and a box of alternate literary magazines. The line stretched for blocks.

76. Christmas Cheer

Mrs. Cecily was so patient. Beethoven's Fifth had an important horn part. Miriam was supposed to play it. She wasn't there. The orchestra practiced other sections, then looked around. Nothing. Next day, she was late. Mrs. Cicely asked if she was OK. Condescension poured out of Miriam. She had better things to do than practice. We were stunned. At the Christmas Concert, the orchestra looked so merry after the horn solo honked and squeaked and failed. They practically cheered.

77. Requiem

Another year ending, and not even the annoying truth was left unpackaged; Pink Floyd's *The Wall* came out and everyone figured they had it pegged. Moe still ran around singing "White Punks on Dope" in German, but an exchange student was shocked and asked if he knew what he was singing. If desperation could breed fascism, if conformity could be an escape, if brutal logic was a double-edged sword, maybe it would cut him out of all of this.

78. ¿Por qué todas las cosas buenas terminan?

Liz hadn't called in a week. No more Spanish homework. The gold chain Tim bought with the money from selling his moped said "Elizabeth." The salesman had talked up the flourishes. Taz turned moped into dirtbike in no time, rushing across yards and fields, playing Hell all over. Mirrors were broken or torn off. The only sweetness was the killing sugar poured into the gas tank by Taz's furtive enemies. So love had ended, and the moped rusted, chained.

79. Dead Fish and Jazz

It was unlike Judah to suggest a trip into the city. He had taught Moe the 12-bar blues, and a lot about jazz bass by then. Moe could probably out-play him; Judah was by far the more confident composer. They headed in to the pier to catch the concert on that bright, perfect day. The air was full of jazz, and the air was full of the smell of rotting fish. Sharp. Their perfect year was starting so well.

@1000thenovel

OK, I can see that writing a novella one perfect tweet at a time is going to be a challenge! K, promise not to start posting it prematurely.

❧

This novel is titled *The Too-Brief Chronicle of Judah Lowe* and is published as serial tweets of 140 characters each so pages are irrelevant.

❧

The Gingko dropped itself a magic golden halo. He stepped as if into a sepulcher, to slowly slam his brow against the dark, unyielding trunk.

❧

Farewell, romance. Moe would not chase Petal around NYU in the Village again. Home he was at a loss, left only with a vague desire to argue.

❧

Fall, and a leap year coming up. What would Moe leap into? He wondered. The town would make a perfect set, waiting for something. But, what?

❧

Moe ran into red-eyed McCoy, who grinned and said, "I have chalk!" Moe wrote "McCoy" in chalk on the sidewalk with an arrow pointing at him.

Not one to leave someone else's idea unexploited, McCoy chalked down "Tazwell" and "parking meter" and arrows pointing to and away from Moe.

As the two boys marked so many things in chalk on the walk to school, Moe only felt more lost. Arrows and labels left a Sesame Street trail.

Morning at McTierney High School, alternately dubbed McTyranny, McTranny, McTiny, was full of teen optimism and despair, crowding the halls.

Nigel Short was the youngest chess player ever awarded the degree of International Master. Moe saw no championships for writing poetry ever.

Morning Math Class. Ms. J. so loved the class to say The Pledge of Allegiance. Moe suspected that she had only read part of the Constitution.

Judah was a year ahead, had the same lunch period as Moe. Judah wasn't the type to skip out for gyros; Moe was more hungry for conversation.

Mr. H.'s biology class was going to be miserable again unless they could distract him from reading the textbook out loud. Best ask about sex.

Here. The cortical homunculus was their opportunity. He was nearing the end of the page. "Mr. H., does this explain why girls like to kiss?"

By the time Mr. H. had discussed kissing and pointed out that nerve sensitivity to light touch affected making out, half the period was over.

Moe never knew why Mr. H. had looked the other way when he drank beer on that field trip. Could it have been the report in iambic pentameter?

Where would it all lead? What did it matter? Latin class was more like Latin Mass, with all of the chanting and repetition. A dead language.

The annoying thing about that English class was Moe could have taught it. Judah caught him in the hall after, insisting on lunch later. Odd.

Mrs. Keny gave a 200-word assignment at the beginning of class. Due next week. Moe wrote it then and there, handed it to her and left early.

Judah was quietly intense. He had a new idea to talk to Moe about over lunch at Gyro Heaven that was so perfect, it would change everything.

Had Taz convinced Moe to try Souvlaki, it might not have seemed such a surprise. It was great. Fresh lamb. The idea? To start a debate team.

Before lunch was over, the idea's magic lit everything with shining new possibilities and challenges. They felt charged with bright purpose.

A debate team only needed two members. The plan's genius part was that the nearby university would have last year's champs: perfect coaches.

For all they knew, it was impossible. It didn't feel that way until they asked Mr. Jameson. No bus. No entrance fees. No coach. Just no way.

Under the moon, they just drove and drove. They had to get home soon. Moe said they could just do it themselves. Wait. What could stop them?

Could they do it? How to know? A call to the New Jersey council made it clear that they would be allowed to. That is, if they could show up.

Key to their plans was prep. They got the topic by phone, ordered materials by mail, and hit the books. Judah's college library card helped.

There were fees to be paid. They feverishly thought of ways to make money, like late-night grocery deliveries to the nurses at the hospital.

From lunch-money to allowance, odd jobs and donations from bemused adults, the fund took shape. It would be just enough. The fees, some gas.

For behold, Israel and Egypt established diplomatic relations and so were great miracles possible, such as Moe borrowing ties to look sharp.

Omar was the math teacher's son. He nodded at Judah in the hall. They smiled at each other. Omar was Egyptian and would join the team later.

Killing time before math, Tim started asking questions about Taz and drugs and rumored parties. Debate Team provided a great subject change.

In time, the plan would be to pile into Judah's car and drive to their first tournament. The snag was finding a teacher ready to come along.

The more immediate problem was the fact that they had no idea what they were doing, really. Souvlakia provided brain-fuel eaten on the lawn.

Souvlakia, ode to a good souvlaki: Maillard Reaction over all, toasty outside, roasty inside, smooth sauce and crunchy lettuce sustained us.

The souvlaki doggerel chalked on the sidewalk gave a laugh at least. Fearing campus security, they retreated quickly into a nearby building.

Artful, beautiful, surprising campus; still surreal to clamber up marble steps, past towering columns and open a thick, echoing wooden door.

Reaching the sanctum, they felt more likely to get busted. All quiet. They walked around: nobody there. Xeroxed posters filled a cork board.

The many posters were about politics, literature, and debate. They had stumbled inside The Most Ancient Plain Dealing and Well Meaning Club.

Started as separate clubs, Plain Dealing and Well Meaning had become one debate society, and the boys lit up with plans to post for a coach.

Just an adult, it didn't have to be a teacher who escorted the debate team! In black and white there in the rules of the New Jersey chapter.

Undoubtedly, it would be a task to find a college student to coach them. But they'd get to judge, when only last year, they were the judged.

Doubt assailed them, but there in the halls of the college itself with the cool flyers they'd take for models. They'd need good typesetting.

Aware that they were looked at differently as teenagers in ties, they started walking differently. Moe found a sharp secondhand trench coat.

Holding his breath, Moe ran into the crystalline cold. In the big lawn there was an old cannon buried nose down. Judah mimed setting it off.

Flailing around for ideas over coffee, Moe's dad overheard them. Moe's dad was in advertising; he could get them some very cool typesetting.

Luck favors the prepared. Intellectual rigor demanded a lot of preparation to be done on both sides of the atomic power and abortion issues.

On the other hand, they could always lose in a spectacular way. The quality of their preparations would gauge the honor to be had in defeat.

Wind and weather mounded leaves across the winter campus. They belonged and didn't belong. They kept their shoes shined and their eyes open.

So things went. It was crazy. Nobody thought it could work. Still, it was fun and they were going to try it if they could. Then, Jim called.

From the beginning, Judah and Moe made light of their differences. Judah teased Moe a little for his moral guide, *Zen Mind, Beginner's Mind.*

Reading: Moe's passion and refuge. He hadn't met anyone who read as much. Theodor Herzl began Judah's canon. They both liked Ursula LeGuin.

On the way to school Moe stopped at Judah's house. Confused silence. Judah's mother had taken a message. It had only turned up this morning.

They understood silently that the message would be purified of association if they didn't speak about it until later. It lived in daydreams.

And they knew that if they rushed up to the public library after school, they could have the public phone to themselves for fifteen minutes.

Ringing the third time, Judah gave the "I don't think he's there" rolling eyes. With a sudden in-breath and a start he tossed Moe the phone.

After the call, they rushed onto the college campus and into the club. Jim was waiting. Cool, even to be made fun of by university students.

But college things had slang names. The Most Ancient Plain Dealing and Well Meaning Club's was 'The Deal.' Jim was a freshman member-leader.

Before he came to the university, Jim had been at Poly Prep in Brooklyn, and had a city edge. Somehow preppy and street at once: hip, smart.

In time they would find out that Jim was also huge. A champion debater and bodybuilder, his neck had trouble fitting into his shirt collars.

Before they could get a word in edgewise, The Deal ricocheted with edgy banter over Jim's attempt at community service with these town boys.

Even then, they could tell that Jim was set apart. Their flyer had been the subject of ridicule. Jim surprised The Deal's clique by calling.

Never were there a pair of buildings on a college campus like The Deal's. Maybe marble buildings, perhaps beautiful, but not a perfect pair.

But what was under Jim's bravado was a kind of blind nobility. He ignored the bad, the negative. Their enthusiasm fueled it, and was fueled.

Elaine was a new variable, distracting. Her blue eyes bright, black hair, pale skin and … curves. The disconcerting gap in her dimpled smile.

Zone, their minds were blown. Jim's dorm number was in their pockets. Who could speak or work yet? It had to be pizza and Battle Zone first.

At least Elaine had honor. She had been talking to Moe, but she agreed to go out with Judah first, and that was settled if still unsettling.

Law, rhetoric, logic, and the creative fact of communication left them amazed at the things they could each say. They quoted famous sources.

Late on weekend nights, they would be cutting out quotes, attributing them and pasting them onto index cards, then sorting into steel boxes.

From Iran, the Ayatollah said the parliament would decide on the hostages. It seemed wrong. The grad school of international affairs buzzed.

Recent events had members of the university faculty quoted in the paper of record. TV crews on campus, like the true center of the universe.

Only Taz seemed uninterested. Moe's little brother had cool projects going on. He and a younger group were making graffiti art of some note.

Moe called from the city. Taz told him he'd pick him up, and to sit on the right of the train. A cartoon face painted on the old coal shack.

❧

Petal called. Moe didn't call back. He opened the letter he'd gotten last week. She'd dropped out of NYU. Her family moved to San Francisco.

❧

Really, Moe thought about Petal a lot, judging by the effort he put into not thinking about her. In and out of San Fran sight of Cisco mind.

❧

All of the time they were preparing, they practiced with Jim once a week. They brought souvlakia from Gyro Heaven and cheesesteaks for Jim.

❧

Gee, I guess this makes us the varsity debate team. Such was Judah's thinking. The two of them were the only debate team that McTierney had.

❧

University security only bothered them once. Despite the many late nights at the café under the religion building, it was in broad daylight.

Even the campus security guard had to laugh. Moe and Judah both simply confessed to being there for the nefarious creation of a debate team.

Moe's theory was that male heterosexuality is inherently transgressive. They just had to get onto that beautiful campus, one way or another.

And then there was Liz. Always there, but accepted to the college now. It seemed to add a cup size to her bra. Maybe it was more confidence.

Days leading up to the first tournament accelerated into blur, but the two debates with college fellows stood out with freeze-frame clarity.

Each time, the frenzy of prep had suddenly stopped for Moe, who'd check the clock, think a half-hour gone, then see only minutes had passed.

At the first practice debate, Jim told the collegians, one female, to show the boys no mercy. The boys showed well, but were clearly beaten.

Girls would be facing them in the debate arena. That was something that hadn't occurred for some reason. They'd also need to recruit: girls.

One came to mind, but for next year. Abortion would be the topic. One very pretty girl had already gotten in trouble for arguing against it.

Let the future take care of itself. The second practice debate had to go well. It did. There was some grudging respect, budding camaraderie.

Everything was setting up. Everything was looking shaky and tentative. Their souvlakia discussions centered in on the concept of confidence.

Maybe battles are decided before they are fought. If so, nobody really can know the outcome before. Thinking you can sure does help, though.

Not that everyone could be trusted. Abscam happened. They got noticeably quieter about their plans at school as the tournament moved closer.

On the dark abandoned coal shack by the tracks, the white lines of a cartoon face. Talk of the commuters, now front page in the local paper.

Taz followed up, with a stranger prank. The puddle of green anti-freeze from the idle school busses was right beside the water-pump station.

All night, Moe practiced ideas and phrases in his mind. There wasn't a real way to rehearse Second Negative's speech. It was extemporaneous.

Going over the speeches: First Affirmative, case; First Negative, beat the case; Second Affirmative, plan; Second Negative, the plan is bad.

Only Taz and his young friends, The 'Tazmanian' Devils knew where they'd got the 'bio-hazard' sign they mounted by the puddle of antifreeze.

You'd think the police would call someone to check before bringing the State and Federal hazardous waste units. McTierney HS's open secret.

Getting ready for the first tournament, Moe tied the silk tie onto his throat. Black coffee and a raw carrot were all that he could swallow.

Until they were driving back with sparkling trophies on the front seat, it all flashed by. First place, plus second and third best speakers.

Years later, Moe would take black coffee and a raw carrot with him before any difficult day. The habit and superstition developed that year.

Unless he was crazy, Moe was sure Elaine still liked him. Maybe it was just to make Judah jealous. She celebrated, but didn't join the team.

Now, the shadow of Taz's exploits loomed large. Judah and Moe paraded their shiny new trophies into principal Jameson's office that morning.

Determined to have a great effect at this meeting, Moe kept completely silent. Judah kept answering Mr. Jameson's questions. He was excited.

Eerie that the meeting should go so well. They had permission for other kids to join as a school club. The trophies stayed with Mr. Jameson.

Really, Moe was slowly pulling away from things already. Deep down, he knew Taz wasn't OK, loved his brother, but knew it wasn't just anger.

So he should have gone to whatever class, but hung around the front archway instead in a reverie. Jerr, a school newspaper reporter, saw him.

Too bad it was caught in print now. "Do you believe in God?" "I am God!" The brilliant caveat discussing atheism was dropped from the quote.

All over the school in the following weeks you could hear, "hey, look it's God!" Somehow smiling Pope gestures turned the jeer into a cheer.

Nonetheless, a lot of kids were asking about joining the debate team. The principal announced the victory over the loudspeaker at homeroom.

Drake asked. He was incredible on stage, and was the solution to their new problem of not having enough time to train kids for the next one.

Even if he couldn't be ready in time, Drake could watch the debates and could ace "Dramatic Interpretation," the theatrical monologue event.

In fact, several of the actors were willing to enter, and the new team members would come to watch. Practice moved to McTierney. Jim walked.

Getting used to being noticed was an issue for Moe. He managed it by developing a meaningful and off-putting smirk. It wouldn't work on Liz.

Hamden Hall, a residential college on campus, was lovely. Brick, Georgian, but faux like everything else there. Liz gazed out a high window.

Twice they'd said "hi" on campus. Moe heard her hushed voice now, distant. He walked out of the streetlight's oval into the dark, toward it.

Yes, this was how Moe came to be perched high atop the darkling and richly-scented pine bough discoursing poetry to the fair and mousey Liz.

Oh, for a ladder. Hamden Hall locked, and he had no university ID. The pine needles pricking Moe's butt were not the only wood in his pants.

Returning to earth, Moe tried to return his thoughts to logic and rhetoric, which were to become his specialties; Judah would take up facts.

So it was in that mood that Sharon found Moe. She pulled over and offered him a ride home. She wanted to speak against abortion on the team.

Only God could know the friction in Moe's mind. He cleared his and explained that debate team members would be expected to argue both sides.

Not that Moe minded running into Liz's mom at the Wawa next day. She just made some jarring comments about divorce and left with her coffee.

Overnight, the family wondered where Taz was, but fell asleep wondering. He dragged himself in, grabbed a shower and got back out to school.

❧

Colt forever, Colt hallelujah, Colt magnificent. Drake's mom and dad suddenly opted to use her car. Drake got the Colt. It doubled the team.

❧

Omar finally wanted to attempt the extemporaneous speaking event and was welcomed. With Alex, they just might thwart McTierney's WASP image.

❧

Mr. Locker brought it all up in class. He celebrated the Egyptian kid and the Israeli kid cooperating. Revelation: Judah was born in Israel.

❧

People were deep. People had compartments. Moe had never heard his good friend Judah speak Hebrew before, just English with a Jersey accent.

❧

Until modern Israel, Hebrew wasn't as everyday a language. Moe learned "silbilm" for headlights came from "sealed beam" car headlight lamps.

The issue of Alex remained unspoken. Did he know they wanted him to be on the team? Could it not be so completely obvious? They drew straws.

Even Drake was nervous. Alex recited Dudley Randall's *Ballad of Birmingham* in the perfect, tender voices of mother and daughter. How to ask?

Ringing silence gripped the room. Alex had taken the stage unnoticed, and then had struck it like a bell. "Is that OK for the poetry event?"

Taz discovered that the downtown parking garage had been be a taxi company circa 1940. From the abandoned office in the rafters, he watched.

Had he known, in the dream, that face, he would have spoken, too. Young and serious, Dudley Randall spoke silent syllables through the rain.

In the week before the second tournament, they had practices, pizza, said, "no thanks" to Mr. Jameson's offer to replace Jim with a teacher—

Suddenly, somehow, they'd made that decision to fail or succeed together. Maybe it mattered less because it had never been done. Maybe more.

"Miracle on Ice" was written all over every classroom's blackboard. Everyone felt electrified. The US team beat the Russians at hockey. Joy.

It was an accidental joke about Ed's house. Even Ed'd laughed. "Ed, you know, Ed, Ed Old Trim. That guy." And he was right behind Jess then.

Let the record show that the trim on the house where Ed's family lived was ornate and decrepit, in mossy purple against vanilla-white sides.

It was not easy to talk to Reuben once he was given a Rubik's Cube. Eventually, he'd put it down in class one day, and never touch it again.

Ed Old Trim was happy to practice improv speaking with Moe. A random subject from a hat, then seven minutes divided between prep and speech.

Under the full moon Friday, their chariots, driving the young actors and speakers and competitors and nerves and laughter north on to Boston.

Alice wasn't letting Moe off easily. She spoke in blurted bursts. Once a week or so in the hall came the shapely, plaid-skirted detonations.

Perhaps they should have acted more surprised. Judah and Moe won higher than any NJ partner team. Everyone placed. Alex took a close second.

Ringing through the halls at homeroom, Principal Jameson's announcement of the win took little sting out of Alice's latest fusillade at Moe.

In Moe's next dream, Jason who was killed in a car accident last year looked right at him. His strong brow was furrowed but he still smiled.

Now there was still enough time to qualify for the State Championships: four meets in three months, placing well enough in the right events.

Could it be possible that they'd die in a nuclear war? Mr. Davits and his improbable toupée took the class to discuss Russia in Afghanistan.

Every discussion of President Carter's boycott of the Summer Olympics reminded Moe that summer would come sometime. Not soon enough, really.

To give PE class its due, here was inspiration for any story satire about totalitarianism. They wore uniforms. Moe's shorts were too large.

Over the next few weeks, they would have to get new pair teams ready. Omar was an obvious choice. Tim was not, but he asked and had promise.

Nobody could have foreseen that the unlikely pair of Omar and Tim — small and serious vs. tall and goofy—would create a major weapon: humor.

Sometimes inspiration comes from unexpected places. Taz saw chalk drawings of a shining baby spending a night in New York riding the subway.

On the crew for Taz's next mural were Tazmanian Devils Dom, Tom, and Brink. Dom, primer; Brink: cartoon; Tom: color. Taz's design and geist.

"It's No Game." David Bowie playing on a cheap plastic box, cigarettes, a joint, lots of paint and primer bought with saved allowance money.

More than the trophies, Moe loved the camaraderie among the team. Kids who were passionate about such different things were coming together.

Almost without noticing Moe signed Judah's team no-drugs pledge. Would it make Jameson happy? He'd signed it but didn't think about it much.

Good thing painting the "Fuck The Government" mural on the garage knocked Taz out. He slept through the fuss below in the taxi office above.

In school there was lots of talk. Taz climbed out of the garage and went down the street. Ice cream for breakfast at The Fred on the way in.

Nothing scheduled today, but Judah called after dinner. The school orchestra would be sending a quintet to a party for Senator Bill Bradley.

Even the most casual school orchestra members lined up to compete to be in the quintet that were going to play Senator Bill Bradley's party.

Dom was visibly upset. His mom grilled him real hard. Moe and Taz were at the Wall. They both knew how to give an ear to a troubled brother.

Home with Dad the Ad Man, Moe critiqued the commercials on TV with him. They paid more intense attention to their semiotics than the shows'.

Over the weekend, Taz and Moe's mom broke out her oil paint and linseed oil as she often did when things got bad teaching Middle School art.

Getting used to the cacology of Alice's anger, Moe oft thought of Liz. College demanded her attention, yet little attention was paid to her.

In the preparing for the tournaments that would count, the debate team lost the interest of The Deal, but Jim hung on. They kept on together.

Even Sharon got into the spirit. She learned a monologue for Dramatic Interpretation, smiling, and helped Drake with Lincoln-Douglas Debate.

How to handle the variety of events that were not always offered at each event? They'd have to learn two or three events. The days were fun.

After school it was dark. The clouds hung low at three o'clock. Moe walked pensively when Taz's Molotov cocktail exploded twenty feet ahead.

Very soon it would get warmer. In New Jersey March was a wet, icy, slushy time. Not yet spring. "Unlocking" as Kurt Vonnegut once called it.

Et in Arcadia Ego. Nobody even knew that Drake's mom had cancer. As if keeping it unknown could stop it. They wore ties. Drake, embarrassed.

Not for long would there be icicles left to taste or a reason left to wear tweed and galoshes. The birds would come and things would change.

❧

After all, Judah's anti-drug pledge seemed to be in preparation for meeting Senator Bill Bradley. Everyone was thinking of something to say.

❧

Day after day real Spring came closer. Their phony Oxford fake was hallowed to neophytes, quaint to the experienced or visitors from Europe.

❧

Underneath McTierney High School, the Tazmanian Devils found the 4' crawlspaces linking incomplete basements. They dubbed them "The Tunnel."

❧

Liz's mom's affair was baffling to Liz. Younger coworker, all the tawdry trappings. Motel meetings. She blurted it all out at once and ran.

❧

To Moe, the campus had seemed a kind of hallowed ivy land. The only ugly building was the Architecture School. But Liz was so unhappy there.

Everyone was surprised by Mrs. Cecily's choices for the quintet. She asked Moe, now a bassist after dropping the cello, to play cello again.

Really, the best players should go. Mrs. Cecily chose for some other reason. Somehow, it worked. I think she asked kids she found political.

Ed Old Trim, cellist, Mr. Locker who was a ringer in the cello section sometimes, Moe, Mrs. Cecily, and the charming first cellist, Charles.

So it was the unusual ensemble of five cellos serenading the donors of Senator Bill Bradley, Charles playing high parts, Moe the bass parts.

Saturday night was scintillating. Surprising. The Senator climbed up on stage after the quintet, spoke, and then chatted with the musicians.

Simple luck helped Moe negotiate speaking with Senator Bradley. It just hadn't occurred to him this could happen so his answers were candid.

Underneath McTierney, the Tunnels stretched from the theater pit to the auto shop. The boys found graffiti from the '40's and one dated '34.

Better even than pizza, Chinese take-out became the favorite meal for debate team practices. It made for sloppy speeches, but it was so fun.

Valentines Day was such a hassle. Every student group sent "cherubs" delivering flowers or lollipops and messages, almost all jokes or rude.

Eros was confusing Moe. Liz's mom's apartment was empty while her mom was at work. They took the bus. It was easy. Something was very wrong.

Reacting to the feeling that everything was pulling him apart, Moe took off to the small Greek pizza place to play Battle Zone. It did help.

Small price to pay. Moe walked all the way back to that Chinese take-out in the little strip mall to get egg rolls without shrimp for Judah.

I think that the decision should be yours – this was how Judah said things should go his way. “Things” were starting to mean one thing: Liz.

Very slowly, Drake came back out of his shell. He was badly strained, so worried about what people thought. It took time, but he kept at it.

Eyeliner, powder, and costume. When the bright light came up Moe could be someone else. Charles directed Ionesco’s one-act *The Bald Soprano*.

Tomorrow was the day to break up with Liz. Then again, the pine tree, again. Then a stolen kiss. Then, tomorrow, and tomorrow, and tomorrow.

How did New Wave get popular in just a couple of years? A couple of years ago the school paper gave away New Wave albums free for reviewing.

Eliminated, Omar was stunned. This Jersey coast Jesuit school was the best they’d seen, by far. Moe lost Best Speaker in a very close final.

Moe read to them, "It is easy, retrospectively, to endow one's youth with a false precocity or a false innocence" from *Brideshead Revisited.*

All the way home, past diner after diner on the Jersey roads, silence reigned. Then Drake said, "We should go out tonight to have some fun!"

Disco roller-skating to "It's A Love Thing" was embarrassing, yes. The ritual bus ride to and from the next town made the skates ceremonial.

Nothing good could come of it. Moe's B+ on her midterm after months of turning in poetry for algebra homework. Mrs. J. suspected cheating.

Everyone took the PSAT: Pre–Scholastic Aptitude Test. Not Moe. Deep inside, threads were starting to break. He could take the SAT next year.

Sweaty under the alert gaze of Mrs. J., Moe did better on the Algebra retest than he had on the original test, eliciting a grudging respect.

"*Sub specie Dei*," the college's motto. Judah developed a funny fixation: deely boppers. He kept wearing them at odd times. Was God watching?

Every day that the sun was bright was a baffle. Like clouds of rain and slush come to sit upon the ground, as if the world were upside down.

Another production of *The Skin Of Our Teeth* at the Playhouse on the college campus turned out to be a welcome distraction. Drake loved it.

To take the edge off of the defeat, Judah pointed out that the tournament was Catholic School League and wouldn't count toward State finals.

Speeches: First Negative, Second Affirmative for Judah Lowe and Second Negative, First Affirmative for Moe Tazwell. Devil take the hindmost.

Omar nominated Judah for Captain. It was always Judah. The present adversity brought out his real strength as they rebuilt their confidencc.

More rumors flew about Taz with the help of the Tazmanian Devils until the legend really hardened. Taz spent days sleeping in while it grew.

Empty ammunition cans, bought salvage at the Army Navy store, helped. Taz buried paints in them under spots he graffitied, before and after.

By late March, the team had two more tournaments under their belt and put so many trophies in Mr. Jameson's office that he built a new case.

Inglorious mockery was hurled at the policeman and teachers who kept capturing Taz but never with paint. It was all buried and dug up later.

Glory had different effects on the team. Some fell into habits and improved. Some not. Sharon quit when her father the minister told her to.

Sometime in the night, the banging began. It startled Moe. He slept when it ended. Taz took out the drywall in his room with a baseball bat.

Another late-night session with Judah's father, professor of robotics at the university. They chewed over the world's situation, and bagels.

Nobody ever caught the boys in the taxi-cab office, even after they started bringing their most intrepid girlfriends. Taz hung up a hammock.

Daring the police, Taz walked by the station carrying a spraycan. But, it was a new and unused one. While under arrest a new mural appeared.

"Wild is the Wind" became firmly linked with Liz in Moe's mind. They started making outrageous plans that they could not possibly carry out.

In May, it was very sudden, surprising, and it seemed instantly that Moe's mom went to work at the university bookstore as a textbook buyer.

Coming home from her new job one day, Moe's mom very casually handed him a university employee family ID card. Would it work at the library?

Happy in a surreal, unreal way, Moe went in a daze from debate practice, to Liz with her roommate out, to the depths of the college library.

Evening was falling and it was magic to drive across the campus they usually walked. Judah told Moe that he was accepted there for the fall.

Something so perfect was so seldom. Moe pictured Judah visiting the team to coach. Their friendship would evolve. Moe planned to apply, too.

Opposite the usual mid-Jersey teams, the McTierney debate squad felt an uneasy mix of complacency and frustration at the teachers' politics.

Frustration made a steady buzz in the background as teammates lost rounds for no apparent reason and looked to Jim for answers. He had none.

In the basement of the university library, Moe pored over the old music scores there. He recognized favorites, and devoured new discoveries.

Really, Taz just thought Molotov cocktails were funny. He especially enjoyed making them out of ceramic knick-knacks he found at yard sales.

Elves with big smiles flew through the air to smash and burst in flames, deer-bottles with big eyes, miniature XXX jugs, all met fiery ends.

Soon the second-period orchestra students were regaled with a real letter from Senator Bill Bradley. Judah was the first to slap Moe's back.

To add to their frustration, they all had to pay dues to meet the team's expenses. No bus yet, no money to help Jim pay for gas or expenses.

Our dreaming of the famous debate High Schools in Florida died with Arthur McDuffie in Tampa, beaten to death by four white police officers.

Now laughter and baking in the basement of the religion building. Nicholas reading *The Hitchhiker's Guide to the Galaxy* out loud. Delicious.

Even Nicholas, so often alone since his four brothers had left home, found these ways to shine. And he gave rides home in his shiny red car.

And Mt. St. Helen erupted. Judah and Moe watched the news, the ashfall. In Judah's quiet distance, Moe noticed how much they usually talked.

Perhaps it was the ash that made Judah consider his feelings of identity, Judaism, and the Holocaust. Moe was so much more an American mutt.

Richard Buckminster "Bucky" Fuller's distinguished lecture was packed. Taz showed Moe a way up a buttress and through a window to a balcony.

Intelligent and canny, Mrs. Cecily used the occasion of the letter to rib Moe in class, bring him back into the fold, the habit of practice.

Laughter was like rain on Nicholas's flower of a personality. May showers kept the basement sought as their own warm, dry, and secret place.

Reading obscure old books in the university library was palliative, surely. Liz gave Moe the name and telephone number of her shrink anyway.

Adam was a late member, and a welcome one. His parents were visiting professors from Chicago. He helped understand the Jesuit school's edge.

In the time it took to get to Rhode Island by train, the team members learned "off-topic" debate: parliamentary with points given for humor.

Nowhere had Moe ever felt as comfortable speaking as in that off-topic tournament. He let it out, wisecracked, had fun and accidentally won.

Stamford or so, and they were exhausted from laughing. Jim had turned red. Judah could imitate judges, other debaters, and the team members.

Maybe Judah's strangeness about Liz would just end by itself. It had been weeks since that good time the four of them had gone out together.

Aviditas vitae. The Tazmanian Devils took crates into the tunnels to sit on, candles to burn, and smoked until a teacher noticed that smell.

Noticing how Liz was dressed usually made her smile. Not so today. She was uncomfortable, so Moe wasn't getting any points for trying today.

In the tunnels, respectfully distant from the graffiti of the 30's and 40's, Taz began chalking up a cartoon for something really ambitious.

Clippings from the newspaper had been assembled on one wall of the biggest room in the tunnels. All of those exploits of the Devils and Taz.

Popping up around town, the face that Taz drew on the abandoned coal shed grinned a silly, happy dead grin. The town had the shed torn down.

Hats became an issue. They tried a lot of them out, alternating styles from fathers' closets and the Hospital's benefit used-clothing store.

A quiet Sunday morning. Cool, but not cold, on the golf course. The sun rose, birds sang. It was the delivery truck that woke Moe and Liz up.

Sometimes it just boiled down to hanging around together, eating and making up arguments and bon mots. Moe could not think up one about Taz.

East River Street actually made an arc right coming from town. Taz ran out of gas on the fast old moped and coasted a straight tangent home.

The weather of the heart, as Dylan Thomas called it, was mere tapping on the windowpane of Moe's conscious mind. He shut that window firmly.

Happy times so recent, so recent that double-date. So warm later in Judah's room. Liz warm in Moe's arms. The girls laughing, and belonging.

Everything was gearing up for the final State tournament. The team practiced harder. Judah said Moe must quit the team or break up with Liz.

Try as he might Moe couldn't make sense of it all. He called Liz. Her roommates brought her to the phone. Even to himself, he sounded phony.

Realizing that he wanted to do the right thing (and mostly wasn't) Moe spent time chasing crazy Wanda. Her figure certainly was distracting.

Or maybe Judah knew that Wanda's "crazy" ideas included wearing high heals and tight sweaters while being completely zealous about chastity.

Underneath it all, Moe wondered how his parents would handle his embrace of Judaism, Zionism really, as he planned. He thought they'd be OK.

Because it all must fit together. Judah had a plan, just no time to explain. No. Judah had no plan for Moe. He was too busy finding his own.

Let me explain. Wanda was not slutty. Her Russian parents had different tastes. To the preppy, WASPy old hive-mind, "different" meant "bad."

Even Wanda's name was picked by her parents to sound more American. She wore fur to school. It would have made sense if she'd had an accent.

Anyway, their breathless haste to seem to act as a couple somehow undermined Wanda and Moe's ability to actually be one. Everyone assumed so much.

Most of Mrs. Keny's class was taken up with the theme of seduction in literary examples. She was baiting Moe, and he knew it. He kept quiet.

Anyway, their brutal tactics in demonizing Moe to the other students only served to enhance his allure. Those teachers were a gossipy bunch.

Yet nobody expected that politics could ever enter the *sanctum sanctorum*, the State Championship Debate Finals. Jim may have but stayed mum.

Moe was glad of the practice he'd done for orchestra. He barely fit in those last few concerts between Wanda's lipstick and prep for debate.

All week, their frantic work for the State Championships made Moe's prep for Student Senate, and Judah's for Congress, seem an afterthought.

Yikes! Just a moment to hear that nobody had ever broken into finals in Student Senate and Congress and Team Debate finals at the same time.

Down to the final round and they were so concentrated on it that they'd almost forgotten the Senate and Congress competitions eating bagels.

And running down the hall from the team debate final to the Senate and Congress competitions infused their speeches with an impromptu blush.

Yesterday, today had seemed a years away. Now, Judah and Moe would fly to San Francisco together as Student Congressman and Student Senator.

Lincoln Douglas Debate, Dramatic Interp, all State events, but only Congress, Senate, and Team Debate went on to nationals in San Francisco.

An average student would have settled for being a sure thing in Dramatic Interpretation. Alex mastered Lincoln Douglas Debate for next year.

Soon, there were newspaper articles and photo shoots to take their minds off of the fact that they beat the pants off the Cherry Ridge team.

Team spirits were not low, just vacant. They celebrated then vaporized. Judah and Moe were left with the consolation prize of San Francisco.

Moe hadn't even thought about where to stay when Judah announced that they'd be staying with Petal's family. He'd asked through her brother.

Over one last souvlaki with them, Jim said that Mr. Jameson had offered to pay his way there, and for his motel. Then, he'd resign as coach.

Moe was so complacent in his assurance that Judah would coach that he didn't stop and realize that deal Mr. Jameson must have made with Jim.

Entirely unexplainable. Jim kept the details to himself, but was very clear with Moe and Judah: they had won the actual debate too, handily.

Now was the time to be pouring over the bills and resolutions prepping, but who cared? They'd been had. Judah got ready for the school prom.

Totally out of the blue that girl who was giving Drake pure Hell ran up to Moe and asked him to the prom. She rented the tux and everything.

Somehow the last week of school presented itself in order, got itself over with quickly, and retired to set the scene for a huge prom night.

Unaware that it would be anything other than stupid – it was actually cool – Moe wore multi-colored Converse high-tops. He bought a corsage.

Suzy had, in one week, found out her boyfriend's money was from selling drugs, dumped him, and booked a role in a play in Greenwich Village.

Almost as an afterthought, Suzy grabbed Moe for the prom, dropped her ex-boyfriend's friends, and made plans for her glorious summer escape.

Nobody got left behind. Wanda had picked another senior as she thought proper. Judah took Elaine, and was surprised to see Moe at the dance.

In the end, a lot was unsaid. Debate team, orchestra, alternate literary magazine, protest poem detractors and fans: all just kids, leaving.

Same Bat Time, Same Bat Channel! Was Drake's mantra. He was a junior. Tim was a junior, said "bye!" to his parents, and hid under the house.

However, the night was not to be over so fast. Suzy had friends from down home at the university. She took Moe to a cool student club party.

Over the music, they shouted jokes about the prom as they danced, and laughed. Jim danced by, and looked surprised. Suzy's friends were fun.

To Moe's ear, they all sounded like hip young residents of Mayberry RFD. The white-columned porch could have been an antebellum plantation.

Summer would have to wait a week or two. The team was again just Judah and Moe, as it had been. In a whirl, Moe packed a cardboard suitcase.

Up to the plane ride itself, Moe hadn't thought of preparing for the Student Senate event, or to see Petal again. Then, he started to think.

Moe was staring at the stack of bills and resolutions when the friendly attendant chatted them up. He asked them to follow him up the aisle.

Moe thought they might be in some kind of trouble or that they were supposed to wait for something in the First Class section. Judah smiled.

Eventually, Moe realized they had been given these massive blue leather seats for the flight. Further amazed, he was handed a glass of wine.

Relaxing and laughing now at the big stack of papers, the boys just marveled at the sunset, joked about things, and looked back at the year.

"Can you believe the team just us again?" "No. Yeah. Wait. This isn't my dad's old car, though!" "And, we're not on our way to … Hackensack!"

Asleep, their arrogance set like wet plaster. Somewhere in the sky over America they flew toward the contest, and Moe's first real hangover.

Moe let it all be a blur, Petal's brother picked them up, they got a burger, they drove through the Berkeley College campus, then he napped.

Petal had broken her foot. She was unusually fully clothed for lying on her bed, anyway. Petal said, "It's been a long time. I'm a lesbian."

Moe smiled and relaxed. "I was beginning to wonder why we were allowed to be alone in your room, you know?" Petal laughed her special laugh.

And, that was the last Moe saw of Petal. Her brother said she'd gone to her girlfriend's house. Moe discovered Guinness Stout in the fridge.

Yes there were late-night poker games at the dorm where most of the student debaters were housed. These were the only things Moe won at all.

Bay Area Rapid Transit and the poker games occupied Moe. Judah actually tried hard to win. Jim had been in town for weeks, visiting friends.

Eventually, Moe stopped going to Student Senate. Days went by in wood-paneled bars, staring outside. Nights became mornings, at poker games.

In time, these memories would take on the inevitable sepia-tones of nostalgia. In the moment, the raw pain of Jim's disappointment was real.

The plane ride back was quite economy class all the way. Judah mentioned he would be heading to a series of camps and meetings all summer.

San Francisco had been beautiful, and the weather, perfect. Summer during the day, fall at night. New Jersey's was summer and summer though.

Only the echoes of things stuck with Moe. For a few weeks, he hardly felt home. He moved his bed to the basement, to give Taz some distance.

Katherine, Liz's twin sister, was home for the summer. She stopped Moe in the street, and asked him to stay away from Liz. Moe was confused.

More to the point Katherine said that Liz had been at the student-club dance and seen Moe committing the cardinal sin of having a good time.

An alliterative allegory all about apples and ampersands alternating aids as anybody's allusions alter an able American's absorbing ability.

You'd think that a campaign of drinking as deep as Moe's would have to go on, but it moderated. He drank at dinner and after with his folks.

Before he could settle down into any routine Moe found that Judah was off at those meetings. But he gave Moe an invitation to one in August.

Eating another apple one day in June, Moe didn't feel like he was learning anything. He felt empty. Taz was growing more distant, and scary.

National Debate Finals had come ampersand gone. The ampersand is a stylized rendering of "et" which means "and" in Latin. Moe felt stylized.

Over and over, Moe's dreams were about asking questions and looking for people and finding nothing. Silence. Emptiness. He'd look for a job.

"Thunder and lightning, very, very frightening," went the song on the radio. So, suddenly Moe decided to apply for a job scooping ice cream.

Only the fame of the debate win and the MacDonald's speech could've accounted for Moe being offered that job scooping ice cream at The Fred.

Katherine, Moe's first customer standing there in The Fred's refulgent parlor, ordered two cups of pumpkin ice cream with one hairy eyeball.

Everyone ended up in line at The Fredericks Ice Cream Shop, called "The Fred," which advertised its own flavors. The line was a social fact.

At first, Moe just showed up, learned the ropes. The shifts flew by in saying "hi!" a zillion times a night and eating ice cream for dinner.

Taz just seemed to sleep a lot. Most of the time. Well, it was summer. Nothing wrong with resting. Moe had learned not to trust the silence.

Somewhere between a family getting blendies and Wanda and her friends again for cups of vanilla, Judah invited Moe to visit his summer camp.

Operating up to speed, the Fred's summer scoopers developed unusually large right arms. Jess laughed and showed Moe her big, developed bicep.

Moe took two weeks to get comfortable at The Fred, and begin wondering why he was hired. The other scoopers were all real leaders in school.

Eating ice cream instead of a meal would become a celebratory habit and joyful mischief of Moe's long after he'd left McTierney High School.

Increasing Moe's unease were the frequent visits of Dom, Brink, and Thomas to The Fred. They acted so forlorn. Taz hadn't been calling them.

Calling was on Moe's mind. He'd called Judah a few times to talk about his summer camp, but Judah was never at home. He'd never called back.

Every time Jess got an order, she laughed a little laugh and went to work. That little laugh wasn't a hard thing to get used to. Not at all.

For a while, Moe kept the idea of Judah's camp in the very back of his mind. Then that Saturday he didn't have to work and Judah dropped by.

Running around the summer-quiet college campus was made more fun with souvlaki. Judah's even better spin on it was: a round of Frisbee golf.

Under the faux-Oxbridge arches, through voids in the modern sculptures, into the base of the abstract bronze which sang like a distant bell.

Somehow Judah managed to be entrancing about his summer camp, and to talk about its meetings and features, without ever being very specific.

The very nature of meaning is contingent upon context. How much more so then when you are seventeen, and that context is chiefly your heart?

Rare were the times that Moe considered his polyglot genetic makeup. Rare were the things that made him think about it. He preferred poetry.

After a day of Frisbee Golf in and around campus, even the orderly, pristine, columns of The Deal seemed happier in their new role as holes.

Too late at night to call Wanda, not that she was picking up the phone much these days. His parents thought he was working. Moe took a walk.

Evening fell. Moe found himself leaning against a big American Elm, in the cemetery. What would those buried here say to him, if they could?

Dumb animal instinct kept him away from home until his parents were asleep. Struggles could wait. There was peace and cool among the graves.

The counselor almost made Moe late for scooping. Moe's debate skills came in handy explaining why he'd stopped coming to sessions weeks ago.

He didn't understand that Moe really couldn't explain it. All of his words: poetry, essay answers and debate speeches, couldn't explain this.

Eating ice cream for dinner again, Moe wondered why Judah hadn't mentioned next year's debate topic. Well, he'd just have to start studying.

The gold Camero rolling by was Antonio seeing who was in line. He knew everyone in line at The Fred. He could have been the ice cream mayor.

Ever since he'd started scooping ice cream, Moe couldn't tell why but Jess acted like she was his little sister, as if she sensed something.

Not everyone liked visiting The Fred on a hot summer night. The lights of Drake's motorcycle passed by a few times, but he never stopped in.

Silent weekday evenings, late at night in suburban New Jersey. When it was quiet at home Moe would open the debate materials he had ordered.

In the university chapel, another flavor of silence was served. Hours before scooping, Moe would sit to think, or at least to calm his mind.

On Fridays, Judah's girlfriend, Elaine, came for a double scoop of strawberry. She said Judah and she had written a few times, that was all.

Not really thinking, Moe met Elaine after work once, and they sat and talked until late. She was easy to talk to and they both missed Judah.

In the late evenings after work sometimes, Moe lay in the basement alone, listening to the radio. Thus he found the college's radio station.

Starting will call-ins to the bored DJ's that turned to witty banter and repartee, Moe started dropping by the station after work sometimes.

By the middle of June, Moe was helping a late-night radio show on Wednesdays that featured old LP's of beat poets, and live poetry readings.

Ultimately the Wednesday night shows were defeated by their own success; it was High School students who tuned in to hear the anonymous kid.

In one show, Moe managed to get The Keither to read an ode to stealing the High School flag and the Assistant Principal to call in about it.

Little did Moe or his parents know why nights were quiet. Taz locked his door, then climbed from the window to sleep downtown in the garage.

Doubtless nothing could prolong that brief, perfect period of solace. While it lasted, Moe got Drake and most of the team on the radio show.

In one show, the grad students in the engineering quad made their prototype voice-synthesizer program call and say, "Play that funky music."

Nigel was a handsome, blond lacrosse player who liked to take photos. Despite events soon to occur, Moe was in that annual scooper portrait.

"Generals and Majors" by XTC. Ginsberg. Talking Heads. Dylan Thomas. A radioskanewwavepoetrygossipparty with ice cream-slick summer fingers.

Careening in as a group, Ed Old Trim's friends pushed him through the door and into the history books of The Fred for eating the most, ever.

How many scoops did Ed Old Trim eat? Every one of the thirty-some Jess put in that stainless-steel bowl. Plus chocolate sauce and sprinkles.

On the Wall of Fame in The Fred, generations of enthusiastic amateur overeaters grin from Polaroids pinned over hand-lettered victory cards.

Counting on the ice cream to hold him, Moe jumped in the car with Drake and Jess one night. They headed to Trenton to hear The Dead Kennedys.

Opening a record "exchange" as they called the used record store was cool enough. They brought that band from the college over. Even cooler.

Lying around on the grass of the benignly quiet summer McTierney HS lawn with a big sandwich from Gyro Heaven chatting with Elaine was nice.

Altogether, only three full radio shows were put out by Moe's *nom de guerre* and his cronies. The Tazmanians helped out. It was a lot of fun.

Then it was over. Oddly, it was Janet the college president's daughter who told the assembled kids of the Assistant Principal's urgent call.

Eating dinner again out behind The Fred, Jess asked to share it, then handed Moe a carved, smoking apple from her lips saying, "smoke this!"

Sweeping his arms in a courtly flourish, and with a witty monologue in a flawless British accent, Moe scooped the boy's ice cream barehanded.

To say that Moe had been fired on the spot from The Fred would have been putting it mildly, not that he remembered anything about it at all.

In the end, Moe woke up on the floor of the chem lab where he used to wash test tubes for minimum wage and went home. It'd smelled the same.

Remembering San Francisco really hurt. Even Moe, numbed as he was, felt losses. He'd liked the bars. He wished Jim had talked with him more.

Ed Old Trim stopped Moe on the street to hope there'd be no hard feelings now. Moe didn't know what he meant. Ed got Moe's old job scooping.

❧

Damn. Leave it to McCoy to rub it in. What an ass. "No ice cream for dinner!" You almost wished him more conceited so he'd only see himself.

❧

Off and on, Moe would pick up the stack of Xeroxed papers, the debate briefs for next year. So cheap. Their cardboard covers, spiral spines.

❧

Forlorn, the papers spread around, and Moe stared at them, and then shuffled them. Nothing happened. No Judah, no laughing, nothing. Silent.

❧

Reading Dylan Thomas was always a comfort. His Mom made fried chicken and somehow the family came together for a good dinner here and there.

❧

Eagerly picking up the phone, Moe was truly glad of Wanda's sibilant chatter. She gave him a surprise invitation to go boating with her dad.

Dreamery, retreat, a magical refuge of arches. The university library was open that summer. Cool depths, where yet no ice cream was allowed.

To a sad afternoon of angsty boating, Wanda's dad added a monologue of commentary. Moe loved boats, he always had. He hated being belittled.

Oral surgery was good to Wanda's dad; it bought a nice Daysailer. It didn't make him fun. One might say the worst part of him was his mouth.

Hopelessly quiet, when it wasn't hopelessly loud with Taz's outbursts. Fourth of July on TV. Home was too stifled for any family trip plans.

Once, Moe glimpsed Taz's room: a busy mess of posters partly covering holes. But his notebooks of annotated collage were just extraordinary.

Temporary rest from Taz's late-night banging and music, the basement almost felt like Moe's own apartment. But only sometimes, not always.

Paneled in that ubiquitous thin and printed wood, the basement was at least cool and safe. Cool and safe also for the family's washer-dryer.

Andover offered a post-graduate year. Moe ordered brochures. This and that at private schools. Somewhere, some way away from McTierney High.

Night in the woods outside of town. The Tazmanians had discovered a room, just a platform in the train trestle. They had candles, and vodka.

Taz was falling apart, and Moe's folks were mostly ignoring it. How to separate his symptoms from teenage revolution? He was also miserable.

So, out of he blue, Drake came by in his crazy old car. It was to say goodbye for a month or so. Moe jokingly asked if he could go with him.

Surprised by his parents' acquiescence, Moe put some things into his backpack and got in the back of Drake's convertible and drove all night.

Waiting for Drake outside a gas station while he paid, Moe felt moist air and smelled dirt and diesel under a bare light bulb. He was South.

In Drake's 1969 Pontiac convertible, you could feel the air change driving up and down the small roads. Lightning bugs rose over the fields.

Moe and Drake had relaxed so much by the time they arrived at Drake's uncle's place, they continued the conversation right into the kitchen.

Insisting that Moe call him "Uncle George," too, Drake's uncle George had waited up, and made the incredible salty wonderful ham sandwiches.

Nodding off and then starting awake, Uncle George apologized, getting up to wash his face in the big sink. He didn't hear the loud knocking.

Howling with laughter, Uncle George hauled his suspenders on and rescued the boys from the incredulous marshal questioning them at his door.

"Only in Sunnyside County! His first name's Marshal! N' he got promoted from sheriff to marshal. So he's the only Marshal Marshal anywhere!"

Laughing, Marshal Marshal leaned back and remarked that their little cousin Drake was now a full head taller than last time he had seen him.

"Evelyn's boy," Marshal called Drake. Evelyn, "Dot's girl," they remembered Dot, the mail carrier. More memories than June-bugs on the porch.

Alvin Krinst was a name the boys had made up in debate team to signal that they were tired, or ready to leave. Drake slipped in a reference.

As the boys begged to finish their sandwiches, they left the men. They seemed to have their own business anyway. Cold Cokes from the icebox.

Resting in the trunk of Drake's car the debate briefs were left there undisturbed. Uncle George had made up two soft beds for them upstairs.

Over coffee early the next morning Uncle George suggested they go see the battlefield, but the boys asked if they could help get the hay up.

New hay had been cut and bailed on the big field beside the farmhouse. Uncle George suggested they should best hurry if they wanted to help.

Because the clouds were moving in and a certain scent touched the breeze, Uncle George asked them to work without breaks. And the heat rose.

Exhausted, not able to raise his arms from tossing hay bales up, Moe sat down with Drake, their backs to the lone tree in the stubbly field.

Noticing the huge grin on Uncle George's face as he brought the tractor through the gate, Moe waved as the grin turned into a shouting laugh.

Moe was about to question Drake when the first heavy drops thumped down onto the dry dust. "I'm one Hell of a farmer!" Uncle George cackled.

On the rising wind, leaves coursed by and the rain suddenly came down in gouts of tub-warm water on the boys' heads as they ran to the barn.

Some time during the day, stacking the hay in the barn or feeding the goats, Moe let his worries about the debate team and Judah rest a bit.

Even though childhood was ending, there was at least a month to enjoy it still, to borrow an umbrella and walk out to the rain-filled creek.

Slowly, the light faded as Moe picked his way over the creek bed, into the woods, to the fence line and back by the barn, glad he had boots.

Beans for dinner, good after their day's work. Uncle George gave them each a Coors. Moe fell asleep on the Formica table before he finished.

Early again, and sore. Eggs never tasted as good as these, fresh from the brown hens out back. The day was going to be clear and hot again.

Noticing the sore spots on his hands, Moe dug in with a hoe and started weeding the garden. It was dawning on him that being there was good.

And it was good to be helping Uncle George. Things needed doing. The chores had added up on him somehow and the unpaid labor was a blessing.

Searing heat built up as the clear blue sky brightened. They borrowed straw hats and kept working, grabbed drinks from the hose until lunch.

Heading back out after sandwiches and Cokes, they worked on through the rows, weeding, until they were finished. Moe wondered what was next.

Entertaining Moe by balancing a hoe on his pinky, Drake almost dropped it as Uncle George drove up in his ancient Willys Jeep, raising dust.

Rumbling down the gravel road until they turned off onto an even narrower dirt road, the old Willys Jeep's metal shell singing each surface.

Reaching a steep incline covered in dark sapphire grass, Uncle George parked the jeep. "We'll leave Eugene here," he said, as he hopped out.

Eugene was the name of Uncle George's jeep and apparently it had been since before Drake was born. The boys dutifully climbed out of Eugene.

Feeling a little awkward, Moe asked what the work was. Uncle George chuckled and said, "too hot ta work!" as he walked into the leafy shade.

Eugene was left behind as Drake, grinning, and Moe followed Uncle George under cool trees and onto the small, rough cable suspension bridge.

Running with long steps across that bridge, Drake got the crossed boards jumping up and down so that Moe had to grab the cables and hang on.

Everything went up and down as Drake's blue eyes sparkled with fun and Uncle George laughed from the far bank. Moe joined in jumping higher.

Now a little dizzy, the boys tottered over the rest of the improbable cable bridge. Drake said they were headed to the swimmin' hole nearby.

Crape and small catfish flickered away under the water's clear surface and into its still, cool brown depths. Moe was caught up by the calm.

Eugene's funny horn bleated a final salute as they drove away. From Drake's cannonball dive, to napping in the sun, bless the swimmin' hole.

To the lazy Hereford cows in the field, summer was about eating. When Moe and Drake chopped up the brush by the fences, they ate it, lazily.

Off and on, Moe kept a kind of journal, started on the blank pages in back of *Collected Poems*, and continued on stray leaves of scrap paper.

Mostly observations and scraps of started poems at first, the loose summer journal grew into notes about using metaphors in debate speeches.

For a Sunday treat, their second week there, Drake suggested going to church with a wink. They woke up very early to drive Eugene into town.

Only the barbershop was open at 6 AM that Sunday, and it was still empty. Moe settled into the cracked and tape-patched oxblood vinyl chair.

Older still than the chair Moe sat in was the barber, stooped but with a clean boyish face, greeting the boys warmly as he washed his hands.

Lost now in time the barber school lesson on washing his hands in front of customers and etiquette. Still, Moe thought, he had learned well.

Entering into his patter, the barber trotted out his prices for shave, hot towel, haircut and shoulder rub in short order and in that order.

Right in the middle of his stock response to Moe's incredulity at the inexpensiveness of his prices, the barber stopped and looked at Drake.

"You sure look familiar young fella. Can't quite make you, though, I'm afraid to say." "I should look familiar, Cousin Jay." "Evelyn's boy."

A strange, twisting white form in a jar of what looked like kerosene stood on the barber's shelf. Moe was probably the 1000th person to ask.

"Boy brought that in and left it here. Never came back for it. Said it was a shark. Caught down by Norfolk at the beach. What do you think?"

You'd have to be rude to point out to a barber who saw WWII that his "shark" was a small dogfish. Moe nodded, looking at the straight razor.

Going from the straight-razored naked feeling on his face to the immediate heat of the wet hot towel, Moe felt oddly relaxed, and cared for.

Over the staccato shoulder-rub, Cousin Jay spoke of Drake's grandmother, "Dot," and how she carried the mail in high heels during "The War."

Now it was Drake's turn. He just wanted a haircut. So Cousin Jay the Barber turned to the phases of the moon and talk of planting schedules.

Eventually Cousin Jay the Barber's mind took a kind of turn away from crops to how the moon'd sink stones in the ground when fence-building.

Evidence in barber Cousin Jay Crowber's experience was that a full moon would sink a stone at the base of an old-fashioned rail fence stack.

Right behind the old, empty Coke machine in his shop, Cousin Jay kept a "genuine musket used in the War Between the States." He showed them.

After the shave, Drake told Moe an old joke about the Crowbers was that the ancestor forgot how to spell "crowbar" 'cause he was "in a bar."

Waiting for the boys, Uncle George mysteriously appeared, standing by Eugene the Jeep in the morning sunshine that perfect Virginia morning.

After the service, people kindly chatted. Uncle George said he and Drake were related to most above and below the ground of that churchyard.

Ronald Reagan would be the nominee for the Republicans this year. It was nice to read the paper slowly on the porch, and drink mint iced tea.

Moe wandered here and there by the farmhouse daydreaming, reading Dylan Thomas and jotting notes for speeches and ideas for the debate team.

Storms rolled through Sunnyside County preceded by a tangible exhalation of the land. You could smell the inner earth if you paid attention.

Evening shadows had just begun to show that Sunday, though, as Uncle George and Drake burst merrily from the barn carrying the picnic table.

As long country summer twilight faded to longer country summer gloaming, Moe was introduced to long country summer eating, of fried chicken,

So near the scenes of so many young men's decisions. Revolution, Civil, 1812, and on, to World 2, Korean, Viet Nam. Young men just like him.

On another hot afternoon, they went to the battlefield near Sunnyside. It was mowed often enough to be discernible but the grass really won.

North and South watered that grass with their blood long ago. Uncle George's telling sounded like the earth itself speaking a rueful memory.

Pepper and salt, Cokes and ham and such. Drake took Eugene into town one morning. So Uncle George set out to walk the fences round the cows.

Ambling over the rise, Uncle George happened to see Spike, their lone bull, rambling off into the neighbor's field and so went back for Moe.

Running as best he could, Uncle George brought Moe along the gated steel chute by the cattle crossing and biding him stay then chased Spike.

It was a still moment, as Uncle George ran around the chute to open the gate. The young bull turned and locked eyes with Moe, who stepped up.

Settling to tell the tale to Drake, Uncle Joe said he didn't rightly know but that he had rushed to killing young Moe, he realized too late.

Rounding the corner and tossing open the gate, Uncle Joe was surprised by the wrong end of Spike. But Moe stood his ground and Spike turned.

Over chipped ice in a tall glass, Bourbon, well water, muddled mint, and sugar. But not tonight. Tonight, straight whiskey was sweet enough.

Calculating up a stopping point, Uncle George suggested they visit the University of Virginia campus that week, and maybe Williamsburg soon.

Keeping an eye on Moe, Uncle George saw some hint of imagination about him, and of trouble. The farm looked much better now with their help.

So without doubt the industry of Drake and Moe had turned some kind of balance in the farm's economy. Some tipping point. A quiet good deed.

❧

Southern charm was further evidenced by all of the cousins of Drake and Uncle George that they ran into, though some were a bit rowdy, also.

❧

Evenings were mostly quiet, reading and writing. They'd independently figured out that Uncle George had a stack of Playboys in the outhouse.

❧

Eating supper one night, Uncle George took up the newspaper and suggested the boys see a movie. They returned to an empty house, quiet farm.

❧

Crunching gravel, a flash of headlights pulled Moe very briefly from his dreaming return to The Blue Lagoon, as Uncle George clambered home.

❧

On the outhouse shelf the next morning, Moe groggily found and started reading a copy of *The Story of O* and it sure did wake him up quickly.

UVA was a beautiful campus, so much more relaxed that back home in Jersey. The Rotunda, marvelous. Moe's favorite part: the serpentine wall.

Slowly walking around the old "academical village," Moe imagined great debates and speeches that had taken place inside its beautiful walls.

In the boxwoods and winding roads of Virginia, Moe felt a kind of calm he loved but could not aspire to, its rhythm both timeless and daily.

Norfolk and Williamsburg were a day of great history and great seafood, Navy sailors all over and a lovely hush over the sheep on the green.

Small souvenirs seemed especially part of where they'd been. Something Virginian about the little blue glass. Drake bought a long clay pipe.

Coming back from their jaunts, they would have a meal with Keith, who came from his cabin in the forest to watch the place for Uncle George.

Or Keith would stay overnight. Slow, there was no telling nor revelation. It just dawned that Keith and Uncle George were more than friends.

Running around in Eugene all over Sunnyside and around they found shortcuts unknown before and drank Nehi Grape when they couldn't get beer.

Notions of arguments for and against a variety of subtle variations on the basic, brutal idea of abortion. Moe's brain, skinned like a knee.

Fridays became regular for Moe to call his parents. Once Taz picked up, and they chatted. Like a call home from some very funky summer camp.

In the cornfield, Moe hit the dirt fast as the crop duster zoomed right over one day. He was making a test pass, and Moe could see his grin.

Eating dinner than night, Robert the crop duster arrived on his BMW motorcycle with the same bug-catching grin on his face and took a plate.

Laughing, they marveled at how bad the wine that Robert brought was. Later, they switched to the Green County moonshine that made Moe dizzy.

Dear to Uncle George's heart were those old records he kept in stacks under plastic bags. He bought good needles for his record player, too.

Soon weeks had gone by and Moe's head and book were stuffed with new ideas. He had a farmer's tan, and lungs filled with clean Virginia air.

Even more precious as his days there came to a close for now, the farm and Uncle George growing better kept and cheerful. A different world.

Mow the yard and by the road and fences, tend the garden, feed the chickens, much to do yet easy for three. Less often some strenuous tasks.

Moe paid for and made a series of phone calls. He'd had the idea out of the blue that a summer debate camp might still have a space for him.

Alley, Drake's first cousin, dropped by one of the last days Moe was there to see this phenomenon, this boy from New Jersey, in their midst.

Waving in the high summer breeze, the cornfield nearby and Alley's lovely hair. She was intense, collegiate, older than they by three years.

Alice was a deep impression, a kind of emotional retina burn that lingered, or a pleasant sting lingering on the skin from a day in the sun.

To be ready for Composers' Club next year, Moe jotted a few themes down. He liked making homemade music paper with a book edge and a pencil.

Sitting on the porch, Drake smoked his long white clay pipe, Uncle George pretended to drink coffee from that mug. They discussed the world.

One more dinner in the twilight on the picnic table. Moe was grateful, said a prayer with Uncle George and Drake and helped with the dishes.

Noting the time in his loose journal, Moe then waved one more warm goodbye to Uncle George as Spike the bull gazed quizzically from his pen.

Julia Child's second book was *The French Chef Cookbook*. Uncle George had her first, and third. Moe found a copy in town to send first thing.

Under the taxi office one morning, Moe looked up at it, and at the fresh coat of grey paint over the garage wall there. Taz was behind both.

Leaning toward routes that avoided The Fred, Moe spent a lot of time on that side of town, reading in the public and university libraries.

Yes, it would be possible to get in to the last session of summer debate camp at University of North Carolina Chapel Hill. South felt lucky.

In his haste to catch up with the debate topic for next year, Moe forgot about the speaking, and soaked up reams of information and opinion.

Smoking was the good, standby way to attach funding to just about anything, really. Who could argue with increasing the taxes on cigarettes?

Going over the things he'd Xeroxed and put together, Moe decided that he couldn't spend any more money. A little left to visit Judah's camp.

One day the town threw a summer fair on the university field, and it was like a day being back at McTierney High School without the classes.

Evening, the fair now over. Moe strolled empty booths. Alice. He saw. She breathed in. He had no defense. She paused briefly. He kissed her.

Dutifully calling Alice the next day, Moe was totally ambivalent to the act she put on for her father, and that she was leaving on vacation.

Alice would find him. He might put it off until school, but it was inevitable. Probably in a hallway, and people would be watching.

Leaving for Judah's summer camp was easier than Moe'd expected. His parents didn't mind. Drake was down South again, with family. Lucky kid.

Eliciting her dimpled grin, a bat squeak of pleasure, and an eye roll of surprise from Elaine, Moe jumped into the back of Judah's huge car.

Kindling conversation on the car ride was unusually difficult. Judah was so stiff that Elaine jumped in to chat Moe up and offer him snacks.

Drawing silent, Moe stared out the window as New Jersey turned into Connecticut. He could almost hear the fun they had once had in that car.

Running through his research mentally as the miles went by, none of it seemed exciting now. He looked forward to talking it over with Judah.

When he finally settled on a fact he thought would provoke their usual repartee and get the debate ball rolling, Judah was quick to beg off.

His face was still. No spark of merriment, no wry smile of possibility on Judah's face, no ready wit. Moe wondered what could have happened.

On the way up 95, they stopped for burgers. Getting back into the car, Moe noticed just how much had been packed into it, and how carefully.

Moe realized then, and from the easy way that Elaine and Judah acted together, that Judah had been home for weeks, if he'd even left at all.

To say that Moe hoped that Judah would explain himself before they did anything or met anyone at camp would have been a huge understatement.

He didn't, though. Judah parked the car, walked Elaine and Moe into the middle of a full camp rally meeting and introduced them on the spot.

Elaine turned so red that everyone just clapped when she waved and smiled. Judah looked at Moe as if expecting him to say something, though.

Reflecting on their ride up, and then suppressing his thoughts totally, Moe made the prettiest speech he could, thanking Judah and the camp.

Finding himself too embarrassed to talk to Elaine at the lunch they were treated to, and ignored by those campers, Moe ate and eavesdropped.

Unless it was a camp for joking around and talking about what college you got into or wanted to, Moe couldn't tell what kind of camp it was.

Could it be the crocheted yarmulkes that all the guys were wearing? Judah had said something about it being a Jewish camp. What did it mean?

Klieg lights brightened the stage, the band played through big amplifiers, the camp show went late, and the three of them slept in the tent.

Early the next morning, Judah got up and told them they could sleep late, that he had things to do at camp and would pick them up for lunch.

After another few hours of sleep, Moe woke up again. He and Elaine ate leftover snack food, and brushed their teeth with water from the jug.

Then it would still be hours before Judah would come back. They talked for a little, read for a bit and dozed off together in the warm tent.

She smiled. They woke up with their faces very close, and kept them there. It was warm. She was soft, smelled great, and made little sounds.

He took a sharp breath in, and pulled his hands away quickly. He went to the tent flap, and unzipped it to sit on his haunches just outside.

In a few minutes that felt like hours, Elaine came outside. She put her hand on his shoulder, and then sat facing him. "What just happened?"

To speak was an effort for Moe. He didn't want to pretend he had finished thoughts or reasons. Just to try to begin he said, "I don't know!"

Not that any of those thoughts or reasons would ever be finished. They heard Judah pulling up the car nearby just then. He came up the path.

On the ride back to camp Judah apologized he'd be too busy to drive Moe to the train station. He had arranged for the camp grocery truck to.

Whatever had happened, what the purpose or point of any of it could have been, Moe struggled but could not make it out. He caught the train.

Now Moe checked out books from the library, and worked in his basement. He cooked, since his parents were working. Taz rarely ate with them.

Alice sent a postcard that she had clearly written for the benefit of her father. And Wanda had decided to write a … not a very kind epistle.

So, Moe got into cooking, taking up his studies where Uncle George's example had left off. He made sauce with roux and soup with a mirepoix.

Sauce Béarnaise was a big hit with Moe's parents. At the library he'd discovered the *Larousse Gastronomique.* He was learning culinary French.

A long time it now seemed to Moe's teenage brain but only three years ago a teacher in a jam put him in a Middle School French class's play.

Under pressure, Moe's part in the French play just made him associate French with older girls and a good accent, like a horny French parrot.

Having cooked his way through a lot of basic French cuisine in a couple of weeks, Moe packed his debate files into a cheap plastic suitcase.

And the duffle bag, and a kiss on the cheek from his mom, and his dad made the long drive to North Carolina, and dropped him at debate camp.

Love is good, but never made anyone perfect. Not the loved, either. Moe's dad gave him a twenty, a tie and a handshake then drove back home.

Lonely and forlorn, Moe climbed the concrete stairs of the empty dorm high-rise and the echoes of his footsteps sounded like Satan's hooves.

By the time he got to that empty room, Moe couldn't have felt much worse. He pulled the old mandolin out of his duffle bag and played songs.

Eager to make up for any perceived wrong, Ernie the head camp counselor bustled into the room and apologized for not meeting Moe downstairs.

God knows, Moe tried not to show how he felt. The painted cinder blocks of the dorm didn't help. The mandolin was borrowed from Judah's dad.

God may know, but Moe didn't know he was OK. He was enough. He had things to share. He felt empty. He told the counselor that he was Jewish.

In the AM, Moe went on down to meet the campers and the rest of the staff. The campers: six other kids. The rest of the staff: one more guy.

Nothing would have pleased Moe more than to have faded into a mass of happy campers and a ton of homework and research. This was so awkward.

"Gosh, Moe Tazwell … a finalist at Nationals in Student Senate had that same name!" was Ernie's rehearsed "funny intro" for Moe that morning.

Going over the debate topic for next year with the kids at his table at breakfast Moe realized that they hadn't studied at all, not one bit.

Over the course of the morning, Moe couldn't avoid the conclusion that he could teach these classes, and better. This was going to be tough.

Doing his best to talk about being Jewish to these very un-Jewish kids as a smokescreen, Moe couldn't avoid letting it all out the next day.

And what came out was art. Moe volunteered to speak both positions, back-to-back, solo, against full teams, then the counselors, both sides.

Letting the madness of his challenge sink in Moe paused. Ernie just asked him why. Moe said it would give everyone a chance to beat a champ.

Letting them all think that he was as unprepared as they were, Moe left the case of notes upstairs then asked for permission to go get them.

Opening the case, Moe laid the index cards in piles. He ordered them with the practiced ease of a Vegas casino dealer, and it all came back.

Very smooth now, "for my first trick," he said, holding a yellow pad, "I will turn this legal pad," he turned it sideways, "into a flow pad."

Everything took care of itself. Moe spoke the way he had enjoyed at the Off Topic event, and used the skills and evidence cards from debate.

Running up to the blackboard after the last debate, Moe said, "OK, here's how I score it," and added points marked in red from his flow pad.

Noting that they would have added points for quality too, Ernie and Justin (the other counselor) gave Moe the win. Lucky they were laughing.

Once the whole thing was over, they went to dinner and then listened to tapes of famous speeches. Pat, a chubby Atlanta kid, chatted Moe up.

What changed everything was when, next morning, Ernie ruefully said that the dramatic art part of camp only had one person. And she arrived.

The music from Flash Gordon went through Moe's head, and it has to be admitted that there was a big imaginary audience in there too. Cheers.

Opening the doors to the lounge on the bottom floor of the dorm, Moe almost ran right into Miriam. She was the acting camp: every bit of it.

Over the next week, Ernie made an effort to add theory, discussion and ideas about hermeneutics to class for Moe's benefit. He needn't have.

Moe had decided to have fun. He spent a day with a new friend, Max, moving furniture from the lounge out into the elevator, and hanging out.

Up and down the elevator, sitting on a couch with snacks on the table and a lamp, Max and Moe talked over the pains of High School and life.

Chasing Max and Moe, Ernie was at a clear disadvantage. They developed a consistent knack for getting out on the floor just before he got in.

Hot nights followed silly days. Moe played the mandolin in his room, far from the others'. Ernie said it was because he had registered late.

For acting a role in real life had so caught Moe that he couldn't stop looking for fun, and didn't notice that Miriam was always around him.

Un-air-conditioned and boiling hot, the campers were alternately languid and giddy at night. On a languid, quiet night Miriam came upstairs.

Nothing came to mind to talk about. Junebugs beat against the yellow bulbs in that torpid air. Moe suggested they go skinny dip in the pool.

Seeing that Miriam was determined and ready to go, Moe set the mandolin down and stepped out. It would be a simple thing to climb the fence.

Up the chain link and down the hill. Miriam was compact, athletic yet soft, tan, proportions perfect. Concentrated girl. And she was French.

Preparing for school in the US was more important than studying acting for Miriam. Disappointed there were so few campers, she still stayed.

Even a late-night dip with a pretty French girl couldn't puncture Moe's silent malaise. Her figure in the clear moonlit water was of poetry.

Really glad they brought towels for the unexpected chills of night and the water, Moe and Miriam kissed then talked about theater all night.

How Moe could be uninterested in Miriam baffled him terribly. And it even more baffled Max, who soon delivered forlorn messages from Miriam.

Over the last days of debate camp, Moe thought very little about debating and took to reading about Israel to drop facts into conversations.

To top it all off, Moe woke up to find a swastika scratched in the back of the mandolin. This was all he'd talk about for the last few days.

Time to leave. Moe thought of Stuart Little and Miss Ames, saying a pent-up goodbye to Miriam. By dinner everyone had gone but he and Ernie.

Yet Moe waited until after they had ordered a pizza and eaten in the silent lounge to call home. His dad had forgotten about picking him up.

Really, it just meant one night in the towering, empty dorm. Moe walked the empty, slick cinderblock halls under reflected florescent light.

Only when he took off the tie his dad had given him did Moe know he was down. Ernie couldn't stay. Emergency numbers hung next to the phone.

After a while, Moe slipped his loafers back on. He didn't feel like unpacking. His steps echoed the empty Hell as he walked to the bathroom.

Deep in the night, Moe awoke from fitful sleep. The next morning, a confused guard watched as Moe exited from an elevator full of furniture.

To Richmond on a morning flight, to be picked up at the airport by his contrite dad who had driven late, and to drive home were pretty nice.

On the drive home, they had taken Route 1 into New Jersey to avoid traffic on the larger highway. Diner after diner, old and new, rolled by.

Returning to his basement, Moe slipped the case of papers under his bed, slipped off his loafers, hung up his blazer and slept for two days.

Unexpectedly, Judah dropped in. He knocked and walked right in. Moe sat on his bed. Judah told him he was leaving, and wouldn't be in touch.

It was hard to speak. Moe couldn't think why he had kissed Elaine. "It didn't mean anything." "Yes, it did. It was a real Moe Tazwell kiss."

Now Moe looked through panes in the door that had just closed to the evening outside's dark green leaves, slanting shadows and orange light.

Bobby was the first person to stop Moe in the halls back at McTierney, to ask about joining the debate team. Moe had hoped he was invisible.

"You should ask your guidance counselor," Moe said, "I heard there's a new class this year." And there was, and some old toupée to teach it.

Opening his locker, Moe was blitzed by last year's team schedule, upbeat pictures from magazines, his poems, and school newspaper clippings.

Numbly pulling things down from his locker, Moe paused to write an acrostic poem, taped it up and slouched off to get his class assignments.

Everything went still for a moment. Moe and Miriam stood, looking at each other across the hallway. She wisely turned and rushed on her way.

Fortunately, pretty Miriam had the real good sense to just pretend she had never met Moe. They never spoke, not once that semester, or ever.

On the other hand, Alice caught Moe staring at his class schedule trying to figure out how so many mistakes could be made. She was so angry.

Right then and there, Moe gave Alice a kiss. She leaned into it as kids whistled and whooped, then she slapped Moe adroitly, and quite hard.

Taking a deep breath, Moe went to the wall near the office to look at the master schedule, and write up a better class schedule for himself.

You should never underestimate the power of being talked about. Coupled with a complete oblivion to it, it can make life very unpredictable.

Miriam was sitting in English class, so Moe turned around and went to Chemistry Two class upstairs. He had enough bad chemistry with Miriam.

Up until this class Moe was considered a "science kid" by his friends. The chem lab students were asked to find the freezing point of water.

Carefully following instructions with his lab partner Tim, Moe stirred the ice and water, dipping the unmarked thermometer. They got "zero."

He was told in front of the class that they must have cheated to get the result. Shy Tim yelled and was sent out. So, Moe swore off science.

It was Danny who reached out to Moe about music. This wiry kid stopped Moe, and asked if he had written that music the orchestra had played.

Seventh period became Moe's quiet haven, learning more about composition. He dropped out of orchestra to avoid politics, friendly as it was.

Taking advantage of his guidance counselor's knowledge of his record and ignorance of his state, Moe asked for the college US history class.

Remembering that McTierney had a deal where the university took students who placed out of the most advanced classes was a last-minute coup.

University policy was to take McTierney students who were still in school but had aced an AP test, or completed the top course successfully.

Even the schedule worked out lucky. Moe would get out of last period to go to the university class so nobody would really know where he was.

Natasha, a transfer, was a new addition to the composition class and a welcome one. She knew a lot of chord theory from playing jazz guitar.

Opening her score to start class, Mrs. Cecily acknowledged both new and old class members, or ‘Student Composers’ as she kindly called them.

Time went by too *molto presto*, but also *molto vivace.* No depth of their ignorance was so dark that Mrs. Cecily would not stoop to light it.

Alex was unphased by the new class, by anything much. He and Emily were a calm unity, hovering over disturbances. Or, they just didn’t care.

Luck not helping Moe, Moe helped luck and stayed out of classes having elections or went late, shaking his head and muttering, “… interview.”

Literary efforts were again Moe’s refuge, haunting the stairway’s bay window ledge. He climbed up to the leaded windows with piles of books.

October would come, and the SAT. Moe figured if he didn’t already have the vocabulary and ability already, he couldn’t get them by cramming.

For Mrs. Cecily, Moe expanded his old *Elegy* piece for the orchestra, adding fun solos for the featured players, expanding the orchestration.

It would have been an easy time, since people were willing to stay away from Moe, or be satisfied with a characteristically cryptic comment.

Taz was attending classes with unusual punctuality. He did his homework, perhaps not brilliantly, but he did it. Something was definitely up.

It was lovely Emily who actually noticed that there something was wrong with Moe. She was gentle about it in Drama class. Moe felt observed.

Nowhere did Moe see anyone who seemed to know what they were doing. These same people acted as if they knew everything. Something was wrong.

A thought dawned on Moe: that if everyone else just like him wrongly thought they knew everything, then he must not know everything, either.

Collapsing all of his daydreams of attending the university, Moe began answering where he wanted to go to college by simply saying, "Paris."

Really, if he was good enough, Judah wouldn't have treated him the way he did. He needed to figure out a few little things, like who he was.

Open to anything, but closed to school for sure, Moe wrote poems people thought were interesting. He joined the peer leadership group again.

Seeing the freshmen faces looking at him expectantly was an experience. Jen was his partner and she was thrilled. They worked well together.

Tuesdays after school, Jen and Moe met to make the plan for the meeting, that was on Wednesdays after school. A clockwork behavioral island.

Innocently asking, "Sorbonne? Or American University of Paris?" kids so worried about their own college chances just got, "Paris." from Moe.

Charlie was out of circulation that month, grounded again for going out singing and playing guitar. He was in composition class now, though.

Nodding her approval, Alice fanned herself with a poem Moe had written that had an acrostic spelling "ALICE." Some were calling it "Moetry."

In Julian's car he had an eight-track player that was out of date in 1980, but he loved it. He had all of the hits from four older brothers.

Giant flowers bloomed over the tarpaper of the movie theater's roof wall. The sketch lines in prep were of grey graphite. It disguised them.

Hamlet is not a type, but a character, which is more complex; less so than a person. And one person can play many characters to many people.

Toxic waste that was fake, a garage mural, now the flower caper: Moe thought it gave their drab East Coast street a shot of West Coast jazz.

Moments, moments, moments, like the September drops on the car window. His dad stopped for Moe to buy Camels, driving to drop him at school.

❧

Almost perfect for granting peace, a cigarette. Especially before school. A smoky suit of armor, inhaled attitude, dragon-breath of courage.

❧

Reading Shakespeare was better than acting, for now. It was harder for the teachers to hassle a kid with a book of Shakespeare in his mitts.

❧

Eating a cheese-steak instead of a souvlaki, Moe began to have the feeling that he was going to have to try to talk to Taz, for some reason.

❧

Solidarity started in Poland. With a great leader, it was the right thing. Moe wished he felt solidarity, and that he could grow a mustache.

❧

Something about dissection enchanted Moe. He took to it instantly. Mr. H. said he'd have him perform for other classes if he could trust him.

Earning Mr. H's trust would not be easy. Moe had a reputation of his own and suffered a not entirely unearned guilt by association with Taz.

After class, Moe asked Mr. H. in earnest to do more dissection. He'd have to sit Mr. H.'s detention with him, while reading up and practicing.

Reading bio and dissecting three times a week made another island for Moe. He could forget everything and concentrate. He truly did it well.

Charlie was out that day, his monthly night, so everyone went out under the train bridge with flashlights and jars of their parents' liquor.

Heading in to Mr. Jameson's office Moe felt hokey. He wasn't really present as the principal complimented their shiny awards from last year.

Heading to Mr. H.'s classroom to cut up a frog, he sympathized. Mr. Jameson's lecture on leadership made Moe feel sliced, splayed and pinned.

After only two weeks, Mr. H. was satisfied of Moe's seriousness of purpose. They put a cart together with a deep dish of wax and instruments.

Rolling a cart full of dead frogs and sharp blades had a surreal appeal for Moe. And it gave him the run of the halls to post up more poems.

During Moe's talks while dissecting frogs for the shocked underclassmen, his wit became as sharp as his blades, so they learned not to joke.

For Jon-O, life was great. He was making more as a carpenter than he thought possible. Nailing walls was easier than playing Space Invaders.

It was a deep need to be heard that attracted Jon-O to Taz's art. He was the first to buy a piece of Taz's, a swirling abstract in charcoal.

Nobody knew how Taz and the crew had gotten onto the roof of that movie theater. Moe knew. The techniques they had developed climbing trees.

Dancing was the only and obvious solution to the McTierney Fall Dance. No need to talk no manners no anything. Moe just danced. And why not?

Now slowly, Moe was changing. He was listening to himself say "Paris." No plan was forming, but intention was solidifying around repetition.

After school one day, Moe went to the library as he often did and got so deep into a pile of books about Paris that he almost missed dinner.

Under normal circumstances, Moe would have found a way to avoid going to McCoy's party. Jen wanted to go together, and so she picked him up.

Getting distance from Jen once she'd had some wine, Moe ended up watching McCoy and a new kid, Mechanic, light up a little glass water pipe.

Habits die hard, once started. Moe had started smoking. He liked Camels, and cool gold and black packs of John Player Specials for partying.

The parties didn't stop either, once they got started. It was frustrating, a game won by money. Moe just had his allowance, and lunch money.

❧

To Mike, Moe's problem was obvious: go to church. Moe asked to try Mike's church with him. No. Mike meant the church for his kind of people.

❧

Olivia was in love. The object of her affection was the band, Duran Duran. She was in Drama Club with Moe. He saw her at all of the parties.

❧

Olivia provided temporary distraction at parties. Then, Moe figured out they were dancing to, kissing during, and talking about Duran Duran.

❧

Letting Mechanic borrow the mandolin when they'd hung around with pizza and listening to the cover of "Ring of Fire" by Wall of Voodoo was OK.

❧

To add insult to injury, McCoy made Moe trade cigarettes for beers at a bad exchange rate. Moe asked Taz along one night to commiserate.

Racing cars to New Hope was a local pastime for High School students, private and public. New Hope had a head shop. You could buy pot pipes.

As an afterthought, Moe bought a cheap but well-designed small pipe intended for Taz when he'd gone to New Hope on the back of Drake's bike.

Casually putting his hand into his big overcoat pocket, Moe found and remembered the pipe he'd bought for Taz, handing it to him sheepishly.

Ever since Moe had hit High School, the brothers only two years apart and once inseparable had drifted apart, becoming friendly but distant.

Smiling, Taz answered the unasked question, and said he liked smoking herb. And he even had a little with him, so they sparked up that bowl.

Nobody seemed to have heard of the pale harmonica player again that year. McCoy had heard his band in a bar in New York that summer, though.

Over the next few parties, Moe conspicuously had more fun with his brother than anyone else there. They laughed and had real fun cutting up.

Then at one party, McCoy got angry at people laughing with the odd brothers, and made a pissy comment. Oddly, Moe didn't speak, but Taz did.

Killing the mood, McCoy's comment at that party made it suddenly silence. Taz piped up with, "you're rich, right? Why is your pipe so lame?"

Eyeing the pipe in McCoy's hand, all Moe could think of to add was, "what else about you is so little, McCoy?" and the boys turned and left.

Yes, the boys had no plan, but the evening wasn't over. They went home to sit in Moe's basement. Taz fetched a glass coffee pot he'd swiped.

Taz had stolen the little coffee pot that room service had brought to their motel room once upon a family trip to the beach. It was elegant.

Over the following hours, Moe's engineering ability and Taz's artistic flair, with a lot of discussion, laughter and ideas, built something.

It was a large and elegant water pipe, with lots of attachments and extras. It was baroque, fully functional and featured a gold peace sign.

Tired at dawn, they lined the inside of a shoebox (for camouflage) with cloth they found and dubbed the pipe code name "The Peaceful Shoes."

A kid who moved away died, his friends said. Hit by a car, wearing his peacock-feather earring. *"Sic transit gloria mundi"* was Moe's elegy.

Drake was in the Fall Musical. He graciously asked Moe to do his makeup for the role, the bald old man, Rich, in *Celebration*, which was fun.

It was the cast party for the fall musical that Moe and Taz chose to debut The Peaceful Shoes, and its ornate design shocked and delighted.

Very jealous of the notoriety of The Peaceful Shoes, McCoy sought out Moe then. For a large sum in cash and a small sack of weed it was his.

Everyone had a lot of fun with the new pipe heading around the party. Moe was already thinking of debuting another new pipe at the next one.

Realizing that his brother was onto something, Taz revealed a cache of outdated lab equipment he'd lifted from Mr. H.'s bio classroom closet.

So, a bunch of design strategies were initiated, involving interesting objects. The Tazmanian Devils jumped into the works enthusiastically.

It was the Tazmanian Devils' hunt for interesting objects to convert to pipes that brought in a run of challenges, from vases to vegetables.

On an easy Sunday, Moe's family sat in the living room, drinking coffee and reading the Sunday Times, and the comics from the Trenton paper.

Noticing the slow but steady uptick in the profits of the brotherly enterprise Moe took steps to formalize everyone's generous shares in it.

Taz had kept his share in his pockets at first, but it was just too much. He filled the coffee can he had hidden under his bed. And another.

Empty, and so confused, if you can be confused without knowing it. Moe took pains to keep his partying confined to parties, but was tempted.

Now and then, Moe walked across the university campus. It would all change back to the bright, merry backdrop it had once been if he got in.

Little by little, the backlog of orders for pipes grew into the shape of a list of dares. For party tricks, Moe would improvise on the spot.

Estrogen is perhaps the stronger of the hormones. Alice was preoccupied enough with her SAT studies to let Moe stay truly forgotten, mostly.

Tangled up in pipes, Taz's art got pushed aside, at least the public part. His sketchbooks lit up with new materials that Moe bought in NYC.

Topography of actual females' bodies was more enticing to Moe than pornography was. Maybe because it was so difficult to buy even a Playboy.

Effervescent as always, Jen seemed convinced that smart planning of the peer leadership meetings would help Moe snap out of whatever it was.

Rolling into Greenwich Village with McCoy one night, Moe realized he didn't know anyone in that car, except that they'd never spoken to him.

"Sutra." The word sounded erotic. The public library had copies of the *Kama Sutra*, shelved beside *The Joy of Sex*, and *Our Bodies, Ourselves*.

Moe hadn't heard from Elaine since that insane kiss, months ago. Walking by her house sometimes, nobody seemed home. McCoy said she'd moved.

Orange and black were the school colors of the college. Moe had bought a tie in them, for nationals. It had brought down a hail of ridicule.

❧

Preparing for the SAT was just not for Moe. Drake stopped him on the way into it. They smoked a joint rolled in purple paper. That was prep.

❧

Rising to the occasion, the boys took in the huge glass vase that Rollin brought to Moe's basement to be made into a pipe. 3' across easily.

❧

Easily drumming up interest in a water pipe for nine people to get high with at once, they had one more flourish: a blow-torch as a lighter.

❧

Stone Soup was the real nature of the game. "Who would like to help fill a bowl that will get nine people stoned at once?" Moe was learning.

❧

Soon Amy was helping smuggle more parts out of the old bio closet. She was Dom's little sister, and very clever. She was the Tiny Tazmanian.

Unbelievable to Moe, almost unutterable were the profits they made. He couldn't buy too much since he was 17. He was too embarrassed anyway.

Revelatory were the things people would do for some of those profits. Moe understood them a little, though. He'd done some stunting himself.

Evolving from simple dares, "stunting" was doing things for collected cash. Moe had taken up a collection last year and jumped out a window.

Rummaging around in the box of things from their old house, Taz found a folder of hospital notes from his mom's troubled pregnancy with him.

Under duress, Jesse, Brian, and Simon pointed Moe out to Officer Thompson as the one who sold them those loose joints. Not that it was true.

Moe was torn. Jesse, Brian, and Simon had ratted him out, and it was a damn lie. But, they had gone straight to get word to him through Taz.

Resting by the smoking wall at school the next day, Mr. Penny came running at the three kids sitting there with Moe. One of them had a pipe.

Under his strict rule of not smoking when not at a party, Moe was not smoking that pipe. He held it anyway so the other kids could run away.

Nothing about Mr. Penny was intimidating or inspiring. He seemed constipated as he looked at the pipe and squeaked up, "come to the office!"

Never mind Mr. Penny's style, he was such a rank suck-up and careerist about the peer leadership program that he was hard to take seriously.

Earnestly charging forward to lead the way for Moe, Mr. Penny went around the corner and most of the way before he saw that Moe had stopped.

Reaching over to his locker as Mr. Penny zoomed round the corner, Moe opened it, tossing the pipe in. Then he stood very calmly in the hall.

"Sorry I lost you with all the kids running around, Mr. Penny. I thought it best to wait for you so you wouldn't think I tried to run away."

Looking straight at the assistant principal, with a straight face Moe acknowledged Mr. Penny's anger and stated that he had not seen a pipe.

On his way in already, Officer Thompson took Moe downtown. There, Moe promptly assumed the lotus position and meditated in the holding cell.

Very much cooperative, Moe asked if they'd like a blood, or urine sample, and was willing to testify about himself, just not the other kids.

Eventually, Officer Thompson just took Moe home in time for dinner. He just didn't act guilty and had no drugs. Mr. Penny would be confused.

Putting the incident into legendary status, Janice wrote a satirical and embarrassing song, singing with her guitar at the next major party.

O. *The Story of O* was right on the library shelf! He'd assumed Uncle George had gotten it illegally, by trading moonshine or homegrown weed.

Relying on his mom's artistic sense and the lessons he took at camp one year, Moe managed to dress Drake up as the old bald man pretty well.

Taz was realizing that getting stoned all the time and showing up at school didn't stop his problem, just slowed it somewhat. Less and less.

Inside the pipes the boys built were interestingly engineered variations on ways to cool and moisturize smoke, some practical, some baroque.

At Drake's next party, a challenge was given their pipe-making by the "garbage can" technique. It made pressurized smoke with a soda bottle.

Overtly, Billy, Tim's little brother, was just a sweet and immature sophomore. He tagged along to parties. Then, it seemed he knew a dealer.

Hilarity met the Jeffersonian system of counterweights that Moe and Taz built into an old brass fire extinguisher to make pressurized smoke.

And Moe realized that Billy was the dealer himself, buying larger bags to cut them up into grams. He'd take orders, acting the delivery boy.

Very soon, Moe began to feel forces moving. His camouflage was wearing thin, but not thin enough for anyone to get close enough to tell yet.

Entire lines of pipes were built. Taz took art classes, perfecting a design whereby a thin layer of clay was sanded away to reveal the bowl.

More than being suspected if he spent too much, Moe also wanted to continue occupying his niche in McCoy's shallow world but not buy a seat.

Even if he finished all of his current classes, Moe would need to take math makeup in summer to graduate. He considered his college chances.

Respite from the daily grind, drama class could still be fun. A very shy, new girl from England named Hope joined. Her dad taught at Oxford.

Canny now, and wary after falling so hard for Petal, Moe actually took some real time to try and be friends with Hope. It wasn't very hard.

Yet fate intervened. The kid directing *The Effect of Gamma Rays on Man-in-the-Moon Marigolds* got mono. Moe agreed to step in, relieving all.

To the dear old drama teacher, neglected Mrs. French, Moe's decision was welcome. "Your work is never a problem, it's getting you to agree."

Reminding Moe one night that rehearsal had gone late, and parents were waiting, Hope was so blissfully, bashfully charming. Moe was smitten.

At least as far as Moe could tell, what girls liked was having attention paid them. So, an interesting girl who liked his attention was key.

Noah could get into a mood where he was easy to talk to. Moe just let it all out, his doubts, ideas. Noah said, "Well did you read Kerouac?"

Since Knute, the counselor Petal sent him to, heard he was studying Zen Buddhism, and had him read Arthur Whane, Moe read, and kept reading.

Getting serious about it, Moe didn't see how Christians had anything to do with what Christ had said. Arthur Whane did a lot of apologizing.

Reading Kerouac, though, it was like a cool primer in independence. Moe cut up an old grey scrap of cloth and made a poncho of independence.

Everyone, just asked Moe where he planned to go to college, the red-haired trumpet player, the rugby player who had a rowing club, everyone.

So the game of answering became a game of planning. He knew it would fail. Knowing it would fail gave him freedom to dream it might succeed.

Such a persistent, if fleeting, dream over tourist books in the library, under a poncho of independence with Baudelaire's *Les Fleurs du Mal.*

❧

Clowning around in the office of the Pangloss Papers, Moe was distracted by the challenge of writing an acrostic poem of the whole alphabet.

❧

Unable to focus as they vied to be wittiest, Moe worked. Reuben barked, "The will to work must dominate, for art is long and time is brief!"

❧

Midnight at a good party. Everyone laughing, pretty happy and loose. A pick-up band played, dub, with a delay. Irma, talking and leaning in.

❧

By talking to her, Moe was again baffled by her perfect skin and that her dad was his dermatologist. She said, "Of course, he helps me too!"

❧

Eventually, Moe managed to mess things up with Hope, too. "Eventually" just came sooner than usual when he arrived with a case of Budweiser.

Reaction was swift and enthusiastic among the Student Composers when news that Marcus the musical polymath was to do a concert of his music.

Lately, Taz had asked the Tazmanians to start asking kids from other schools if they needed water-pipes, or small clay pipes. It grew sales.

After a brief session in Taz's room trying out a new pipe, Moe let Taz know that any sales he wanted to do with his clay pipes was all cool.

Not all brothers would say this, but Taz said that all of this business started with Moe's friends' parties, so they should split this, too.

Doubting now that he really had any true friends other than Taz, Moe spent a whole entire weekend asleep. It was strange. He woke up hungry.

Moe took some time to come up with a Plan B. It was depressing but there was always the Army. His dad had served. It might be fun to travel.

On another day, Tim's dad tried to find out what was wrong with his son. No scientific magazines, no interest in his microscope. Teen angst?

❧

Nodding slightly on a bench in town one bright autumn day, Moe was startled by a college man asking if he could sit. It was the cool singer.

❧

Kakistocracy reigned. The offices of the Pangloss Papers were emptied over the weekend. Copies in the school library were all that was left.

❧

Exactly why the little room was cleared out became obvious as the nerds who hid there wandered around while substitute teachers took breaks.

❧

Yet, Jen would soldier on, meeting in a classroom instead. The 'Papers got a funky new faculty advisor who wisely kept a hands-off approach.

❧

But, it was not the same for Moe. Nothing was. He got a real glimpse of what it used to be every once in a while, which truly made it worse.

Under the tree, on that bright autumn bench, the cool college singer and Moe had spoken. They both agreed that the unknown must be hazarded.

To say Moe's confidence in his plan went up as he put cash into the coffee cans that hid in his box springs would be a lie. He ignored them.

Topping a nine-man pipe was never going to be easy. They made a watermelon pipe, and some concealable ones. They didn't have a machine shop.

For Halloween, Taz was more open this year about his plans, and Moe joined in. The idea was to scare the Hell out of anyone who was a bully.

Learning some of the new tricks that Taz had made up for graffiti work, Moe scrounged up black cloth for camo. They hid caches of supplies.

All over earlier than they expected that night. They protected little kids who didn't stay out late, the victims of the older kids in packs.

The tactical key was to find the dark places away from adults, potential problems, and the usual bullies who were too old to trick-or-treat.

❧

Unreal, wild fun, throwing Molotov cocktails, close to frighten but not harm, eggs, misdirected with noise and gave little kids time to run.

❧

Laughing about and recounting their exploits with the Tazmanians on the way back, they stopped as Suzy pulled up in her VW bug to say hello.

❧

Eventually, they went to Moe's basement when they were tired of standing around Suzy's car. She brought candy, and a bottle of peach brandy.

❧

Now I can't use a real person's name here. Alvin Krinst would kill me if he found out. I'll have to come back to fix this, use another name.

❧

Could it be that it doesn't count if I mention the name but don't actually use him as a character? There will be experts on this to consult.

E Pluribus Unum. A bunch of misfit kids, a little tipsy from brandy, and a cool girl to tell stories to, so they left happy. And she stayed.

Putting Suzy back in her VW the next morning, before his parents woke, Moe began to ask. She'd stopped him. "I've got to go back to school."

Under the trellis, orange leaves and black shadows. The train going over. And the geese, honking, commuting between pharmaceutical campuses.

Sunday, Mandy called him up. And he went over for tea. They drank tea, among the large dolls that her mom made, and Moe played their guitar.

So, of course, in school on Monday McCoy had questions about his "tea" over at Mandy's. She sure could make him jealous, had been for years.

Friday, Judah's dad waved to Moe from the car they had driven to the debate meets. Moe said he'd call, his own voice sounding leaden, phony.

In Drama class, Moe threw himself at the improvisational games. His goal was always to subvert, send up, lighten up. Anything but the truth.

❧

Laughing at the new kids flailing around onstage, Drake and Moe chatted about the shows they'd done. Drake avoided asking about Moe's plans.

❧

Little helped Moe laugh now. Some things, mostly when he was alone. The parties felt phony, people, empty, McCoy's trips to New York, false.

❧

Even pot was getting uninteresting. It made him feel like he just wanted it to wear off as soon as he smoked it. Drinking was good, numbing.

❧

Despite the fact that Taz seemed better at school, it was hard to ignore the short, spitting bursts of rage just under his breath sometimes.

❧

Putting a little money into his account cautiously, Moe took a money order into New York and got a passport made. That was a long, long day.

Having stalled and put off meeting Mr. Jameson for days, Moe finally went on in, expecting a talk about motivation or his grades, or debate.

And it was, in part, what Moe expected. Mr. Jameson also made a confusing plea for Moe to consider going into politics. This seemed strange.

Kabobs, on a New York City street corner. "Dog meat," his dad called them. Moe was daydreaming about them. Mr. Jameson mentioned US History.

Over his Sophomore year, Moe had taken Advanced Placement US History, and done well on the test. It was the tail end of his childhood mania.

So Mr. Jameson told Moe that New Jersey law required that he take US History 1, which his test score qualified him to teach, or fail school.

Considering this the day that he dropped out of school, Moe had smiled, and said he understood. He was told to go to the guidance counselor.

Over the next few days, Moe found that the poetry had turned off in his head. He established a pattern of going to the few classes he liked.

Poetry, poetry, poetry. Where was its source? Moe wracked his brain late that night in his basement. Every poem he started seemed stillborn.

Entering Moe's window "office," Miriam of the horn incident, then Jeb, the junior drug dealer, said that Mr. Abel, the counselor, wanted him.

Reading the Wall Street Journal in his window had gotten a teacher or two to scratch their heads. Moe read that Princess Diana was pregnant.

Opposite the main campus, set near the golf course, the seminary was a secluded place. Calm, except for the nights when the bar got rockin'.

Mechanic smiled and brushed Moe off. Not in the mood to chat then, Moe didn't think about it. He had meant to ask him for the mandolin back.

After Moe's mom backed the car into a post, he was glad that he knew Rodney, a senior who had graduated and was working in his dad's garage.

Now, out of the blue, Jimmy, Charlie's little brother, showed up at school in a Rastafarian scarf. He seemed worried without Charlie around.

After school, Jon-O drove by in the old pickup truck he had bought. He gave Moe a ride and suggested he meet Mr. Hightower, a friend of his.

Copying down the dialogue from his notebook, Moe briefly considered that this might not be a great time to try and write a musical. Why not?

Lying across the couch that was in the set on stage, Moe explained to Mrs. French that the characters represented emotions, only abstracted.

Everyone was nice about putting up Moe's one-act musical, but it was terrible. He saw that, they all did. They did one after-school showing.

For a week, though, it had felt like better, at least at school. Moe hid in the library, and the costume closet, reading. It was comforting.

Dropping class one morning, Moe walked a coffee can of cash over to the travel agent, and bought a plane ticket to Paris for New Year's Day.

Eating pizza at the Greek place, Moe saw Tammy and Jack come in for sweet baklava. It was cute. He bought it for her, and she fed it to him.

And the peer counseling members were starting to look at Moe funny. His attendance at leadership meetings wasn't good, and Jen was covering.

The erotic thoughts that came to Moe's mind were hard to suppress, as Jeb and Jen had obviously been talking about him just as he walked up.

He hadn't stopped to think until now, looking out of the library window, that maybe the tax on his cigarettes was paying for something good.

He didn't want to run into Jim, anyone he knew or who knew him at the college, so he stopped going to the campus library, the campus at all.

Ersatz coffee, an herb and toasted grain mix, had leant its distinct, bittersweet odor to sessions in the basement of the religion building.

Luck was not going his way that day, and he ran into Jim outside the Greek place. "What's happened? People ask me about you."
"Wish I knew."

Later, Moe decided that he'd learned something from Jim and he worked on getting in shape a little at a time. And it was a habit that stuck.

Over McTierney High School's archway, "LEARN TO LIVE, LIVE TO LEARN" was etched in a gothic font. "With yourself, by yourself," Moe thought.

Appropriately, Spencer (the rugby and rowing guy) played the handsome lead in the fall play, Agatha Christie's *Toward Zero*. Moe was drafted.

Being a character who smoked a pipe, Thomas Royd, was fun for Moe. What was odd was feeling more like a character at home than on the stage.

❧

Calling the prop pipe "The Thomas Royd Bowl" at parties was fun, since the whole cast seemed to end up at all of them. Ms. Christie was hip.

❧

Dragging out his best BBC imitation, Moe also helped the other kids with pronunciation and soon the whole show took on a fairly English air.

❧

Eric was a rock drummer who took up jazz and couldn't find anyone to play with. Moe did. They played the Bolling *Suite* after play rehearsal.

❧

For Spencer, the character of Neville Strange was perfect, because he was the very last person anyone would ever expect of murdering anyone.

❧

Going after the Bolling *Suite No. 1 for Jazz Flute and Piano* without flute or piano was an act of faith – faith well placed in Mrs. Cecily.

Happy to embrace Janey, who played Kay Strange in *Toward Zero*, Moe noticed her smile, her heat and sweat, and that she wasn't wearing a bra.

In the end, they played the Bolling *Suite* after school. The kids liked it. Then Parents' Night, and holiday parties raising orchestra funds.

Janey had broken up with the boyfriend she'd dated since elementary school. He'd been cruel. So you could say she used Moe, but he liked it.

"Kake" from the vending machine in the teacher's lounge was all Moe could afford for dinner, before rehearsal. He did have a few cigarettes.

Letting her mind relax, Jen thought about the past year and what had happened. The Space Shuttle would be used again. But could Moe Tazwell?

Meeting Mr. Hightower had been a strange experience. Moe was flattered by the old man's interest, and surprised that it seemed to be sexual.

Nobody saw it coming, but Sylvia, a sophomore, snagged the lead role in the Spring Musical. Everyone was shocked, but Moe congratulated her.

❧

Opening the production of *Toward Zero* was fun and a surprising success. Drake played Superintendent Battle so well. Three good performances.

❧

Parties were good, or bad, big, small. Drake's parents weren't home Sunday night. *Toward Zero*'s cast party was legend: the biggest and best.

❧

Quiet Ben brought in a chamber work for the Student Composers Club; the third of them to sport a trench coat, and now the most accomplished.

❧

Reading in the public library, Moe looked up, his head still wrapped in Seneca's words. Looking down, he'd realized that Liz had been there.

❧

Slowly looking up from his book, Moe found that Liz was not there. Her pale, staring figure, arms crossed over a that blue jacket, lingered.

Turning to the window, Moe already knew that Liz was both smart and furtive enough to go out a way that he could not see if she'd wanted to.

Under the High School, the tunnels became a very comfortable hideout for the Tazmanians. Dom's dad beat him, and he practically lived there.

Very soon, Mr. Tremont and Mr. Bell, school social workers, were taking some undisguised interest in Moe. They were asking around about him.

With Taz sleeping all the time, flaring up in inappropriate ways, and destroying things for no reason, Moe thought the counselors were off.

Xanthippe was Moe's "X" word for the alphabet acrostic poem that he wrote for the Pangloss Papers. Jen asked for a poem, on peer leadership.

Yet Moe went to the meetings. He did enough to keep out of real trouble, and asked for help. They wanted to talk about him, not his brother.

Zoon politikon, Aristotle's political animal. Moe had no taste for maneuvering so-called adults into believing him, if they did not want to.

❧

For the Christmas Concert, Moe politely begged Mrs. Cecily to be let go. He was doing too much even if it wasn't what he was supposed to do.

❧

Upstairs, Taz kept Moe's mom and dad tired and enervated. Moe's dad drank more scotch than usual, more often than he had. His mom was quiet.

❧

Catching Moe in his window office, Ed Old Trim asked about some debate terms. They talked about last year. The team all hated the new coach.

❧

Keeping his eye on the courtyard through the leaded glass, Moe spoke with Ed of the many things that Jim had taught him and Judah last year.

❧

At school, Moe overheard Mrs. Jenkins, a substitute teacher, complain of buying a cello for her son. Moe offered his old one from the attic.

Behind the record store, Irma took a smoke, asking if he was Jewish. "Ish. Enough to be burned, not enough for your dad to let me date you."

Asher, Ben Asher. Judah was home for a short break and asked to meet Moe, but with his friend Ben Asher from camp with them, too, on campus.

Not prepared for the meeting's subject, Moe followed Judah. They walked over campus as he lambasted the abstract sculptures. Moe liked them.

Death visited the theatre. Mrs. French passed around the newspaper story about Lotta Lenya and said Brecht would never be allowed at school.

On the walk around the sculptures, their old Frisbee Golf holes, Ben Asher flowed at a distance. Judah asked why Moe had not called his dad.

"No reason," was all Moe could say, tongue-tied by Judah's abrupt and hostile tone. He should have said he wanted to talk to his old friend.

It was an unpleasant evening, leaving no sense of conclusion for Moe. He walked home over the cracks in the concrete feeling vaguely guilty.

Nothing on Thanksgiving felt exactly right. It was as if a great tragedy had occurred, hushing everyone. The Lions beat the Chiefs 27 to 10.

Getting back home on that evening, Moe saw their neighbor, Mrs. Bass, by their side door smoking a cigarette in her house-dress and slippers.

And Taz locked himself in his room, the windows wide open, and wouldn't come out, playing loud music sometimes, shouting, hitting the walls.

November, ending. Phil and Jeremy, nice guys from the new debate team, asked Moe to come along to the next meet. So, Moe thought, "why not?"

A miserable weekend of bad speeches in the dramatic interp event, strange looks from his old teammates, and sneaking off to get high ensued.

Lovely fall evening, that Sunday. Moe returned to his mom crying, his dad silent. Taz had been arrested for staring into neighbors' windows.

Yes, Taz was locked up. McTierney House, a minimum-security facility. There were outpatients. The police took him there, instead of to jail.

There was still Battle Zone and a slice, the Greek or Italian places, across the street from each other. It was almost the same, for the moment.

It wasn't easy, and Moe's mom and dad said they couldn't all visit Taz for a while. The doctors said he needed time. Maybe in a week or two.

Casually slipping in questions about Taz, McCoy invited Moe over that weekend. His mom would be in NYC, or somewhere. Moe slipped out of it.

After school, the Tazmanians came to Moe's basement. Moe drank a pitcher of mostly vodka and a little orange juice, vomited, and passed out.

Letters in red ink on pale pink paper that folded up into an envelope: Wanda, whom Moe had all but forgotten, apologizing for forgetting him.

Wanda. Something had gone wrong, and it had to do with the boat outing with her father, Moe thought. He couldn't put his finger on the leak.

A dream about old Blackie, their dog, who had died when Moe was little, featured him singing, dancing, and speaking incomprehensible French.

To Moe's dismay, James the known pyromaniac, came up to him in the hall, acting like they were old friends. Mr. Abel was probably behind it.

Eating in the school cafeteria felt like a novelty. The Big Duke was sloppy, not as bad as he remembered. Then again, he wouldn't miss them.

Reading again, into travel books about Paris, Trixie stopped to talk. She was tall, but the picture of the Pixie that had been her nickname.

Trixie was a peer leadership person, so Moe was wary. She did not mention it. She talked about his poetry, and a speech he'd made last year.

It was strange, this tall, pretty girl who looked like a cartoon sprite being so intense, as if she had just woken up from a spell of sleep.

Going up the street, into the cold evening as it fell, Moe called his folks to say he'd be out. He ate soup with Trixie. They talked, a lot.

How could he have known what she'd say? She asked if he remembered the newspaper story from last year, about the rape on the college campus.

Turning to look at Moe in the dim light of her porch, Trixie smiled, but Moe could see she was crying. "Moe, the girl in that story was me."

The hooker's name was "Silk." She was polite and well-spoken, helping Moe call a cab, and get in into it. He was in Trenton, somehow. Drunk.

Ending the day by sleeping through his stop, Moe sobered up a little walking back to the right junction. He'd miss the last town train, too.

Not ready to face the school he spoke with Knute's office who sent him to Frank, a county "counselor" who turned out to be a truant officer.

December. So many eyes that looked away, eyes that had been looking at him a moment before; with the sideways, breathless, bug-eyes of fear.

Eyes looking at him and his eyes looking at empty pages. He labeled each page in a notebook "Chapter One" writing them all. It was terrible.

Reading was still an escape, more so with the house so quiet. They moved around slowly, as if in mourning … the smiles few, very far between.

Leaving town now had a furtive air of daydreaming. There was a Kurt Schwitters exhibition at the Guggenheim. The *Guernica* had left New York.

Onions, garlic, fried in a little olive oil, with mushrooms and herbs, the heat turned off, cream cheese blended in to fill a lonely omelet.

In a silent way, instinctually, Moe cooked more. Like an animal huddling by a wounded fellow, he sat dinner in front of his parents, silent.

Noticing that T.S. Eliot had died two months before he was born, Moe reread the poems of blatant genius, yet somehow bloodless now, distant.

Counting on a weekend of distractions at whatever parties McCoy was throwing or sponsoring, Moe was vaguely surprised to be off of the list.

And George had graduated the year before, gone to India as rumor had it, instead of university. Dean, George's sophomore friend, called Moe.

North wind and rain raged outside as George sat restlessly in Moe's basement, seemingly blown in. Dean had cryptically arranged to drop him.

Dean had made a point of avoiding questions about the meeting, or George's reasons for it, even if it was George's idea or Dean's, or whose.

Yet, Moe got the feeling that neither Dean, nor George himself knew why he'd wanted to see him. Moe suggested they take a walk and find out.

Cascading rain took on a hushed feeling as the blustering winds went still. They walked, under black umbrellas. George needed him to listen.

Over the months since he had gone, George made his way to India. He volunteered at an orphanage. It left him feeling broken, a real failure.

Letting him tell his tale, and spend his fury like the wind, Moe led George into the park outside of town. They stood by the stone monument.

Or did George know he was angry? Probably not. Moe asked gentle, easy questions. Did the children smile? Did he do his job? Did he complain?

Released from his own self-judgment George had laughed at how angry he'd been. Moe called him a hero. Not much else was said that rainy day.

Bouncing around on stage and joking, the drama kids were on a kind of early vacation. Nothing would open now, making way for holiday events.

But Alice smiled at him in the hall. Of course, the rumor followed fast that she was dating Chris, that tall peer leader guy. What a relief.

By now, no one spoke to him about anything much, so he knew little about the debate team. He'd heard that Tim and Omar were doing real well.

Under the stage, an entrance to the tunnels was hidden by a stack of lumber. It seemed a million years ago that Taz and Moe climbed in here.

Leaving school early one day that December, Moe found himself in front of McTierney House. He stared at the walls, walked around, and cried.

Everything in Taz's room was as it had been when he left. The walls were full of holes, thick with glued magazine photos and marker writing.

Boring in a way, and nonsensical, manic, the scrawled words in black marker on the walls still seemed urgent. Desperate, insane, incoherent.

Under the excuse of driving Moe to the store for clothes, his dad took him away while his mom tore down all those pictures, words: evidence.

Taking unneeded time looking at shirts, Moe was overcome by hunger. His dad agreed and they went out to hamburgers and chocolate milkshakes.

There was not a lot to say about Taz. They were worried, surely, numbly sad. They haltingly discussed Moe's grandmother, who'd been treated.

There were Soviet troops massing on the border with Poland. Moe would cry a lot, when he was drunk. He had a lot massing on his border, too.

Racing through the assembly of some new pipes with complicated cooling mechanisms, Moe's heart wasn't in it. He called Dom to come get them.

Opening up a box in the garage, Moe found another stash of Taz's clay pipes to hand over to Dom, pretty, swirled porcelain, and terra cotta.

Prepared for something like this, Moe was still surprised when Steve, the fresh new peer counselor kid, invited him to the semester wrap-up.

How Mrs. Findley justified using her students as PhD guinea pigs was entirely her business. Moe expected better than the humiliation he got.

Yet he brought it on himself by going, and left abruptly when the criticism took a turn toward the Piggy-killing from *The Lord of the Flies*.

Year of the Flies, maybe, or of lies. Not that anything was easy enough to point a finger at, to blame. No end of it, and nowhere to put it.

Even Drake had grown distant, literally and figuratively; school-bussing in from the next town, his family moved. There were other problems.

America, America, God shed his grace on thee. The whole world could not be this way. Right or wrong was not the point: different, elsewhere.

Reading Camus in his basement, Moe was called upstairs to the phone. Uncle George sounded concerned. He went back downstairs to Dostoyevsky.

Solidarity was not having a good time in Poland. Moe was not sure what of his ideas were lies he told to himself, nor why he was not insane.

Unitarianism sure did sound good. Moe visited the church and was approached warily there by Lisa and Veronika, both honors English students.

Perhaps because he'd expected something pure, the Christian slant and watered-down Protestantism of the Unitarians' funky service irked him.

Even the materials of the service were odd to Moe. There was a wok filled with cat litter, into which a lot of candles were stuffed and lit.

❧

Regretting that he couldn't feel sincere, Moe tried to make up for it by being polite and interested. Lisa and Veronica were alert to scorn.

❧

Maybe everyone looks funny doing certain things, like having sex, or going to church. The Youth Group meeting after the service was relaxed.

❧

After that, Moe set out on the walk home, but Lisa's family picked him up. A big family, the car bounced happily and noisily up the streets.

❧

Noticing that Moe was quiet, Lisa tried to sympathize. It was hard not to grin with the kids playing and laughing. Moe smiled. It felt good.

❧

In the pretty light Lisa brightly said that they'd love to see him in their church again. Moe wistfully thought about Sacré-Coeur, far away.

Coming home to his own family's ritual of coffee and the Sunday New York Times all over the living room floor in progress, Moe settled down.

❧

Counting out Q-tips to take to Taz, toothpaste, pajamas, little things. The situation reversed, Taz would have added comic books, and candy.

❧

On the last gig of the jazz flute and piano group, they played the Bolling *Suite*. The tipsy hostess wanted more. They got up and improvised.

❧

Mary was the duty nurse, tired, but patient with their questions. Taz was resting. He could not see visitors until after seeing the doctors.

❧

Plowing on with daily life, Moe thought about taking the tickets back to the travel agent, but didn't. They were pressed under his mattress.

❧

Letting his hand move over the small bodies of his stuffed animals, Moe remembered the colorful adventures he and Taz had designed for them.

Inside the box with the little stuffed animals were a few shards of the control panels, drawn with felt-tip markers, for shoebox spaceships.

Moe pulled the little animals out and lined them up, recalling the names, personalities, histories, characters, distinct tastes, and voices.

Empty of Taz's sounds, the house seemed also empty of something vital. There was no correspondingly happy music to replace the violent noise.

No snowmen would be built of this slushy snow, no snow-ice-cream made, or sledding performed. The only virtue of this cold wet was solitude.

They got to see Taz, in the visiting area. Usually not more than once a week. Sometimes, every few days. He had good days and some bad ones.

Christmas. They knew what was coming. Moe's mom cried. Taz would be sent to a secure facility after New Year's, though he seemed calmer now.

A day before Christmas Eve, the doctors let Taz have a pass for that night and Christmas Day. A nurse called and their dad went and got him.

❧

Really, my abiding impression is that Taz was heartbroken, scared, and sad. He knew who he was, what had happened, but couldn't remember it.

❧

Busty and wonderfully naked from the waist up, Donna was Jeb's girlfriend. When she'd answered the door, she had clearly been expecting Jeb.

❧

On Christmas Even, Moe gave Taz the proceeds from the last pipe sales. He didn't ask if he could have it there, or what he would do with it.

❧

Nothing seemed quite right, but they did giggle a bit from smoking the weed Moe had bought from Jeb. They settled into the Christmas ritual.

❧

Christmas was coming, and at least they'd be together to care for each other, and they knew, vaguely, that it mattered, would always matter.

Over the streets and shortcuts they had run wildly around at Halloween, Taz and Moe walked quietly. They were both remembering, not talking.

Pausing at a no-man's land fringe of bushes between houses and a small park, Taz wondered if memory would prove as unreliable as perception.

Yet Moe was not only remembering the older kids they had scared away from hurting the younger ones. He was remembering, too, their planning.

"Kakes" from the Wawa, cigarettes, peace and quiet, and meals with the family: Taz didn't ask about art supplies or his friends those days.

It was Christmas. What do you buy for your sad brother locked up in a loony bin? Moe visited the campus chapel. He just decided on sweaters.

Lying in his room, the walls stripped bare, Taz was tired, vacant, and wan. They listened to the radio, talking about childhood Christmases.

Leaning against the wall of an empty McTierney High School, Moe smoked by himself. Taz was napping at home. David, balding at 17, walked up.

It occurred to Moe that David was the preacher's son, and he remembered that their house was near school. He didn't preach; just said hello.

Night and silence. Taz often slept, exhausted. His problems weren't brought up. Quiet and concern reigned, as if he were getting over a flu.

Going out for a cigarette late at night, Moe noticed some freshly turned dirt under Taz's bedroom window. He turned back inside, forgetting.

He found the nonsense going through his head comforting somehow, and went upstairs for a glass of his parents' rum. Merry Christmas, anyway.

In time, he would look back on this as an important moment, he felt strongly, and the seeds of the future just beyond the corner of his eye.

Moe shaved his head for the first time. Before he went back that day, Taz helped him. The interim stages provided humor, a momentary solace.

I do not think John Lennon would want The Dakota remembered as where John Lennon was killed but rather as where Yoko Ono lived. Dec 8, 1980.

In Ionesco's *The Bald Soprano*, the play starts again after it ends, with the actors switched. Yet, the play was performed. That's different.

Intensely placed between regarding the Divine and thoughts of death, basement reading Shakespeare, still the only infallible escape for Moe.

Interwoven with Moe's thoughts now was a search for some thread, in Seneca, Shakespeare, Watts, in life, all that could see life as freedom.

Interlocked with his thoughts of freedom, Moe found very little in ideology that had any distinguishable value, so many vectors to identity.

Inspiration for action was so bittersweet, and unpredictable. And once found, it possessed the immediately melancholy air of future history.

❧

Interest in Taz was hard to ignore. Kids had parents who worked in the hospital and knew people at McTierney House. Misery was great gossip.

❧

Introspection only led to the idea that the only safe place was death, the only normal thing, in the end, that to which we must all conform.

❧

Incubating the little idea that travel could lend a linear progression to his wandering thoughts, making his body adventure as his mind had.

❧

He couldn't hate his friends' writing. Moe put his poems in an envelope; tied it tight. Maybe someday they'd seem like they were a friend's.

❧

Now President Reagan added an embargo on trade with the Soviet Union. Moe could sympathize with being embargoed. The phone didn't ring, much.

On the last day of school before the Christmas Break, Moe had stayed all day. People who wanted to chat would turn up, classes were relaxed.

Winking at Moe as he sat in on bass for orchestra and chatting him up in Composition class, Mrs. Cecily seemed to have some hunch about Moe.

Brideshead Revisited on Masterpiece Theatre with Jeremy Irons. Music. Moe considered carrying a teddy bear. No. Something ugly would happen.

And Mechanic hadn't been in school, or answered his phone for weeks. Moe asked around. Moved to his dad's in California with Moe's mandolin.

Nothing consoled Moe in the coming weeks and months like thinking of composition class and Mrs. Cecily, though he would never see her again.

Great. Mrs. J. had heard of Moe's good SAT math score. Her compliment was to imply that he'd cheated. He ate pancakes, and hoped she'd leave.

The pancake house was an intersection of town and gown. Chocolate-chip pancakes possess universal appeal, of course, for teens and twenties.

❧

He felt like he'd get busted, on the white steps of The Deal, eating a hot cheese-steak sandwich. Steam from the sandwich rose to disappear.

❧

Entering the long street of student clubs, Moe felt like a matador, felt the moment when he had faced down the young bull at Uncle George's.

❧

Lost, but finding a new sense of purpose, Moe felt like he was sleepwalking. The jet's wheels hitting the runway in Paris would change that.

❧

Over the course of the day, Moe packed and unpacked the big duffle bag. Then, he took out the old debate case, and emptied it of its papers.

❧

Now on his bed without their case, the briefs and notes for a debate case never made looked as abandoned as they were. Arguments never made.

Laying the briefcase beside those papers, Moe blew the dust off of it and put a few essential things into it: socks, t-shirts, Dylan Thomas.

Evening, and quiet. Sleep for Moe's parents. He wrote a note, and placed it beside his ticket on the bed. He picked up the ticket, and left.

Yearning for some way to bring back the day, to eat a souvlaki and plan the debate team; surrendering that he could not and should not care.

Driving over the dark New Jersey landscape on New Year's Eve, with its holiday lights, he imagined the bus a spaceship, the lights as stars.

Really, Moe had the vague feeling that the *Bildungsroman* he told himself about himself had gone so badly. Could he rewind it like a Walkman?

Under Pressure, David Bowie and Freddie Mercury sang. Moe looked out the jet's window. Black: a blackboard to write on or ink to write with.

Moe would not hear from Judah again for thirty years. The End. Thanks for reading, and may your New Year's Day start an adventure this year.

About the Author

Christopher Carter Sanderson is the author of several play adaptations, including the adapted works of Tucker Max, *I Hope They Serve Beer On Broadway*, and a one-act version of Alfred Jarry's *UBU IS KING!* His scholarly work, *Gorilla Theatre*, is published by Routledge. The New York Times, American Theater Magazine, The Village Voice, Jezebel, and others have all critiqued his work since 1994. Mr. Sanderson is a dropout from Princeton High School, a Fulbright scholar, a graduate of programs at New York University and Yale University (where he is an associate fellow of Calhoun College), and a professor at the State University of New York, Oswego. He is married to Meredith Kadet Sanderson, and co-parent to Charlie, a rescued Jack Russell Terrier.